THE *Song* *Bear* OF THE

MARK TUNGESVIK, MD, JD

WESTBOW®
PRESS
A DIVISION OF THOMAS NELSON
& ZONDERVAN

WestBow Press books may be ordered through booksellers or by contacting:

WestBow Press
A Division of Thomas Nelson & Zondervan
1663 Liberty Drive
Bloomington, IN 47403
www.westbowpress.com
1 (866) 928-1240

ISBN: 978-1-4908-7388-6 (sc)
ISBN: 978-1-4908-7389-3 (hc)
ISBN: 978-1-4908-7387-9 (e)

Library of Congress Control Number: 2015904154

Print information available on the last page.

WestBow Press rev. date: 05/08/2015

To Nathalie

PROLOGUE

Germania in the Year 5 AD

Thirteen centurions stood at the ready looking out at the pitch-black field that lay in front of them. It had now been several years since the light of day had broken through the dark canopy above. As their eyes adjusted to the dark, they could make out the even plain that seemed to stretch to the horizon. The dirt was smooth, as if someone had recently tilled and sifted it. Behind them was the tree line of the forest, where all vegetation stopped sensing the curse that laid on the soil beyond.

They stood fifty yards apart at the tree line, each holding a spear in their right hand, a small knife at their hilt. Their armor, helmets, and shields lay neatly stacked behind them. Their master knew that their armor would do them no good, so they had stripped down for speed and stealth. Other than their sandals and a piece of cloth wrapped around their waist, the only clothing they were allowed was the hide of a wolf worn as a cape, with the head of the wolf over their heads for a hood. It was a sign of their loyalty to a higher power.

Behind them glowed the red eyes of the giant wolf. Twice the size of a horse, the wolf looked out at the dark plain that lay ahead. His eyes were much keener than the men's, and in the distance he could see the reason for their sortie deep within the forest. In the middle of the plain stood a dark tree thirty feet wide that rose like a pillar supporting the darkness above.

In the minds of the men he gave the command to go. Starting at a slow jog that soon led to a full run, each took off into the darkness. They were allowed no torches for their own protection. The wolf looked down at his forepaws, which were covered in lacerations that were slow to heal.

He had thought himself immortal before entering the field before, but now he was not so sure.

He turned his attention back to the men. They made a good pace. Kytann, the great wolf, led them through their minds, keeping them on target. He looked off in all directions but saw no movement other than that of the men. They were to go to the black tree and carve out a piece of wood from its trunk, large enough to fashion a spear, and then return. The task was simple enough. Kytann gave them a one in ten chance of surviving.

As if to confirm his odds, he heard the cry of one of the soldiers. His eyes focused on the spot of the scream and there he saw the shadow of a great beast. A shiver ran down the wolf's spine as he watched the beast tear the man apart with no more effort than that of a strong wind tearing off the petals of a flower. The beast moved quickly across the plain, clearly homing in on the remaining men. Kytann redirected their paths, but even without their armor they were not fast enough to evade the beast, as their screams in the dark confirmed.

One after the next his men fell. With each kill the beast seemed to gain speed. There were only four men left now, but the fastest had nearly made it to the tree. It was then that the beast stopped dead in its tracks, as if sensing something more horrible than itself was watching. It turned and ran for its home deep within the caves on the far side of the plain. Kytann followed the beast with his eyes, noting which cave it disappeared into. He then redirected his focus back to the men.

The first soldier to reach the tree took out his knife and ran his hand over the bark, looking for a crease to begin cutting. The scream he let out thereafter chilled even Kytann, as the wolf watched the flesh from the man burn away as if acid had been poured upon him. The sight so shocked the great wolf that he was not able to warn two of the other men before they, too, touched the tree and fell victim to its curse.

One man remained. Kytann ordered him to freeze in his tracks. He needed time to think. He had not anticipated that the tree itself would be so toxic. The man stood fifty yards from the tree when the earth began to tremble. The very dirt seemed to come alive as it vibrated. Kytann knew what was to follow. He turned and headed back into the forest. The man's scream only seconds later confirmed that he was not protected from the monsters that lay deep within the earth. Perhaps if he had more men …

But Kytann realized that, in reality, he did. He had an entire Roman legion at his disposal. He would return with more men next time. The thought of the shadow beast disturbed him. He would need to learn more of the cursed beasts that guarded the black tree.

CHAPTER 1

Sixteen Centuries Later, in the Black Forest of Germania

John stood in an open field, watching the evening fog weave through the wall of trees marking the edge of safety. He stood tall, just shy of seven feet, with shoulders as broad as those of an ox. His heavy arms, built strong and hard from a life of labor on the farm, hung loose at his sides. Coal-black hair flecked with grey swayed to a somber rhythm on his shoulders. It wafted across a heavy black beard with a hint of red that had woven itself into years of neglected growth.

He took a deep breath. The air was damp with the promise of spring, and the musk of winter leaves fallen long ago filled his nostrils. In the distance, a shape appeared and then vanished like a shadow, moving along the edge of the forest circling the meadow.

John could feel the heaviness of his boots in the wet ground, and his stomach churned as he tried to turn and run—but he could not. His black trousers and work vest encased him as if he were wrapped in iron wrought from the depths of the earth. His white shirt billowed in the breeze as if to feign the movement he could not muster.

The moon made the fog at the edge of the trees glow. And through those fallen clouds, the head of a great bear slowly emerged. The muscles on its face rippled like waves on the ocean. He was three times the size of any bear that John had ever seen. His legs reminded John of tree trunks.

He met the bear's eyes with his own, his feet frozen to the ground by fear. He felt naked. Barely able to breathe, he felt his heart torn between two unfathomable desires—one to break from his frozen state and run, the other to abandon safety and approach the bear.

Suddenly, the fog swirled around the majestic beast, and the great bear lowered itself like a spring on a trap. All John could do was watch.

It was then that he awoke. The dreams were coming almost every night. John rolled over in bed and looked out his window at the tree line across the meadow. The fog still lay thick on the ground, but there was no sign of a bear. John had walked the tree line a thousand times and never seen any sign of bear tracks—only the scattered tracks of wolves and foxes.

Much of the forest was far too dense to explore. The trees hemmed the clearing in like a wall, with thick thorn-covered vines weaving tightly between them. The dense mesh of tree and vine hung like a veil over the forest, hiding secrets from those who wished they knew what lay beyond. Only the smallest of animals and the wood grouse that flew overhead would ever know what lay hidden in the darkness of the forest. Ancient paths made long before John's birth crisscrossed their way into the forest to places only legend spoke of, for no one dared to follow them into the darkness. None who had wandered those trails ever returned.

As a boy, John had crept into the woods farther than anyone in the village would dare. Uprooted stumps and wolf tracks were all he had found. If there was life on those paths, it was well hidden.

After yet another dream, John looked out at the forest and wondered what lay deep in its heart. Although he had not followed the trails very far in when he was young, he had noticed that they veered away from the center of the forest. No bear could move through those tightly knit trees—not even a small boy, as John well knew. The bear of John's dreams would have left tracks deep within the mud of the forbidden trails.

John's house looked more like a massive barn than a house but it was typical for his village. Sitting far out of town near the forest's edge, its side walls stood only six feet high, but the massive thatch roof sloped to the sky nearly four stories in height. The house was more roof than wall. The three-story western side was the house's only tall wall. On that side was John's makeshift bedroom.

The structure backed up into a hill on the east so that the upper level where the hay and grain were stored had ground access. This was also the site of John's huge workshop with a small area with a bed in the corner where John slept. He had designed the middle level to be the one where the family would live, with proper bedrooms and an open kitchen. But John now spent as little time as possible on that floor, still haunted by memories of the past. The lower levels where he kept cattle had easy access to the pasture on the north and the south sides of the structure.

John could hear their soft sounds below him as they woke. He told himself there was no bear, and yet the thought lingered. He wondered whether he was slowly losing his mind.

As if to confirm that thought, Betsy's bell began ringing as the cows began to moo their morning greetings to each other.

CHAPTER 2

Four Years Earlier

The sun shone bright on a midsummer morning, peeling off a thin layer of dew that still held tight to the flowers of the meadow. A cool breeze blew over the field. Waves of blue and lavender rolled across the edges of the meadow like the surface of the ocean as the wildflowers bent to the will of the wind.

In the middle of the field sat a small woman in a blue cotton dress. Her golden hair shone bright in the sun as it blew to the rhythm of the breeze. She leaned back and closed her eyes, imagining the master's brush laden with bright reds, oranges, yellows, and blues as it fell upon the earth, painting his never-ending portrait on the canvas of the meadow.

Becky opened her eyes and smiled as she looked across the field. In the distance, she could make out John's massive silhouette at the edge of the plain as it met the forest. It was there that the bright colors of the meadow gave way to the pale blossoms of the lilies that grew only at the forest's edge.

They were Becky's favorite. She could easily pick them for herself if she wanted, but John took such joy in bringing her a bouquet mixed with the blue flowers that she never ventured to the forest's edge. She looked on as John moved from one patch to the next, particular over each stem he cut, mindful of the loved one for whom he labored.

Becky reached next to her and grabbed the cowbell that she had taken with her. Her voice wouldn't carry across the field, but John would hear the bell. She rang it, and John's head popped out from behind a bush like a startled deer.

It was Sunday morning; they would be going into town for church and to pick up supplies for the farm. Becky strolled to the wagon that she had already tied up to George, their only horse. John had owned him long before they were married only three years ago.

Becky gave George a hug as she patted him on the head, and George nestled in closer as Becky scratched behind his ear. She climbed up on the wagon and watched as John bounded through the colors of the field, bouquet in hand.

John had worn his Sunday clothes to pick the flowers. Becky smiled. His trousers were covered with dew and pollen, and his white shirt was soaked at the collar with the sweat of his morning labors. As he drew closer, he was smiling ear to ear. He was in his mid-thirties, but his smile was that of a seven-year-old boy in love for the first time.

Overflowing with energy, John reached the wagon. "I bet if you wanted to, you could pull that wagon to town by yourself," Becky said. She smiled and patted the seat next to her.

John bounded up as if love had granted him a first date. He handed Becky the flowers.

"John, they are beautiful." Becky smiled and kissed him on the cheek. "And you found the blue flowers that match my dress."

John smiled and shook the reins. George happily trotted away from the field and down the dirt path that led to the village. It took most of the morning to reach the village, but John hardly noticed. He cherished these morning rides with Becky every Sunday. He would talk of the animals that he saw in the forest and the funny shape that a tree may have made growing around a rock. Becky would quote a piece of a poem that she had read the other night. John would lose himself in imagination as Becky's voice filled his mind with pictures of a world far beyond the farm.

John chuckled to himself. It was scandalous for a woman to read. John and Becky did not speak of it to their neighbors because others thought it was such a ridiculous custom. The only other person that knew that Becky could read was Father Aeneas Brown, the local priest who had taught her. He had been a good friend of her family before her parents died.

John left his thoughts behind as they arrived at the church. There was Father Brown waving them over to greet them.

Becky held out her hand. "It is good to see you on such a beautiful day, Father Brown."

Aeneas smiled at Becky calling him by title. It was their code for Becky needing another book to read. Aeneas helped her down from the wagon. "Why don't you show John the stained glass while I get something for you?"

Becky led John up to the little church and took him around the room, telling him the story that was portrayed in the colored glass. She did this every Sunday, as Aeneas had done with her as a child. There were only ten stained glass windows in the church, but John never tired of hearing her voice. John would stand in silence as the melody of Becky's voice seemed to merge with the bright colors streaming through the windows. Color covered John's body, and he felt the warmth of the sun on his face. If he lived a thousand years, he would not forget the joy of this day.

The sermon was short. Aeneas had made the handoff of a small package wrapped in cheese cloth after the sermon. John then took Becky for a walk down the narrow streets of the village. There they would buy pastries and cheese for a picnic later that afternoon once they got home.

There were fewer people walking up and down the cobblestone streets than usual. Many of the shops were closed. Aeneas had spoken of a sickness that had been passing through the village and had offered a prayer for those suffering from it. John kept himself between Becky and the passersby, not wanting her to get too close to anyone who might be sick. But there were other reasons, too. He and Becky had not been able to have children yet. He had seen the longing in her eyes as they passed children in the street. He could not bear to see her reminded of a barren womb, especially today, on their anniversary.

As they casually made their way up the narrow street they saw a small wooden ball rolling toward them, bouncing here and there as it hit each cobblestone in its path. Following not far behind was a young boy who still wobbled when he walked. The ball bounced near Becky's feet and as it did, she swooped down her hand and caught it. Having built up his momentum from the run, the little boy was unable to stop, but Becky caught him in her arms.

Up close John thought the boy's long curly blond hair made him look more like a bush than a boy. Becky pulled back his hair to see his face, which promptly turned beat red as Becky set the boy down and placed the ball in his tiny hand.

Behind him John and Becky spotted a man bounding down the street. When he reached them he was clearly out of breath but still smiling. He reached down to pick up the boy, breathing heavily. "Thank you, ma'am." He coughed as he rose and then made his way back up the street with the boy in hand.

John said nothing of the boy for the rest of the day, not wanting to upset Becky, but she did not seem to dwell on it. They made it back to the farm in time to eat their picnic in the meadow. The sun was now setting, filling the sky with golden pinks and deep blues. Off in the distance they could hear thunder. A storm was coming.

John reached around from behind him and grabbed a package he had picked up in the village without Becky seeing. Becky smiled and graciously accepted the box. A tear fell from her eye as she opened it to find the dress in the store they passed by every Sunday. John knew she had tried not to let him know she liked it; it was too expensive for them to afford.

As she laid down her bouquet, she said, "Look at this, darling. The flowers match the colors in my new dress perfectly." She kissed John and told him that he should not have bought it, that George was getting old and the money would be better spent on a new horse.

John would hear nothing of it. He then took out the book that Aeneas had loaned them. For the remainder of the night Becky read poetry to John, and John's mind drifted into a world painted by Becky's voice.

Later that night Becky developed a cough. Initially John thought it might have been from the flowers and took them out of the house. He could not have been more wrong.

CHAPTER 3

Four Years Later, the Morning after John's Dream

John pulled himself up to the side of the bed. He wiggled his toes in the wood shavings that covered the floor near his bed like pine needles in the dense forest. Even at forty, he was more boy than man. Some of the pine shavings were fresh from last night and filled the room with the scent of the great trees. Becky had loved the smell of pine. John looked down at his makeshift bed, which was nothing more than a hay-filled mattress tucked in the corner of his workroom and wondered how it had come to this. He had lost Becky to the sickness that had passed through the village three years ago today. He had given up sleeping in their old bedroom, overcome by grief by the mere sight of the bed that she had died upon. He had closed the door to that room after Becky's funeral and had not opened it since. With John's parents having died in his teens, John now found himself alone, with only cows for company.

John stood up as if to ask an imaginary partner to dance and then began to waltz through the wood shavings. He had never been much of a dancer, but Becky had loved to dance and now these early morning shadow dances were all that he had left to remember her by. John twirled around the dozen workbenches that filled the huge room. Flocks of carved wooden birds looked on from the benches as John gracefully danced his way through the shavings. Piles of cuckoo clocks in various stages of production lay strewn on the many benches, the product of a man drowning himself in work to keep his heart closed off from the weight of the world. Today

John would allow himself to open that place in his heart if for only this one dance.

He had already learned that some things opened are not always easily closed. A wound of the heart clumsily locked behind the door of busywork would only hold so long before it pried itself open, yearning for a deeper healing. Like a man throwing buckets of water from a sinking ship, John had sensed that the miniature mechanical houses were not enough of a distraction. This realization had led him to begin the grander project of mechanizing his entire house. Great gears and springs loomed in the background of the hayloft, connected to the far reaches of the house by pulleys and belts that had taken several years to devise and construct. In the upper floor alone ran over one hundred pulleys with ropes and belts disappearing in holes in the floor. The largest of the ropes overhead ran from the machine toward the double doors that opened into open air three stories high. There the rope went over a pulley and dove down to the ground.

The distant sound of Betsy's bell brought John back to reality and with a boyish grin on his face he ran toward the open doors and flung himself out to the rope that hung three feet from the outer wall. John held tight, as he did every morning, and he began to descend as his weight pulled the rope down. He met the counterweight halfway down moving in the opposite direction. He had carved it to look like one of his cows. As he let go a cog shifted and the carved cow's full weight pulled down on the rope, thereby winding the giant clock that was his house.

John waited for a moment as the lower doors to the stable opened for him. Water had already started pumping into troughs near each of the eleven cows in the barn. The cows were known as *hinterwald* cattle and they were common to those parts. They stood just shy of four feet tall with short legs that let them graze on steep slopes without toppling over. Each had a white head and a yellowish tan body, except for one, Betsy, John's favorite, who was a dark red brown below the neck.

Betsy wore a bell below her neck to let John know where she had taken the rest of the herd in the meadow. She let out a loud "moo" at the sight of him and he smiled. John sat down to milk Betsy first. Looking above him, he could see fresh eggs on a scooped conveyer belt heading up to the kitchen. John looked on in pride as grain fell through shoots in the ceiling and Betsy bent her head down and began to eat. He chuckled to himself at what a visitor might think of the sight of the wooden brown cow hanging from a rope high in front of his house. It was good that he had no visitors. Less awkward questions to answer.

When he had finished milking the cows, he looked toward the stairs that led to the middle level of the house. He had designed the machine of the house so that he could spend as little time as possible on that floor, but that was where the kitchen was and he needed to eat. As opposed to the soft browns of the stable below, the kitchen was adorned with various shades of black. John's kitchen, like others in his community, had no chimney. In the middle of the windowless kitchen sat a fire pit. Wood from above had already fallen into the stone ring and bellows ran by mechanical arms to stoke the fire. Smoke rose up to the ceiling boards, creeping around the soot-caked wood toward the thatch roof above. The room was saturated with years of smoke and soot. Salted pork hung from the ceiling, which in time would mature into smoked ham.

A door from the back of the kitchen opened and a life-sized wooden likeness of Becky emerged with a frying pan in hand. Shortly after her death, it had seemed a good idea to incorporate Becky into the kitchen. Maybe seeing her likeness will ease my loneliness, John had told himself. Instead, it had had the opposite effect. "Becky" was dark with soot, moving along a track in the floor like a miniature figure in the cuckoo clocks above. In her pan were two fresh eggs that she swiveled and placed over the fire. As always, John reached up and cut off a piece of meat from an older ham hanging on the ceiling. His days had turned into a routine that varied little from month to month, much like the figurine of Becky cooking eggs in front of him. He stared down at his tracks on the floor. They were just as worn into the soot as hers.

The fire's light bathed the hams hanging from the ceiling, casting shadows that looked like wolves dancing in the night. His feet were not affixed to tracks in the floor boards as Becky's were, but was he any freer that way? *What if all the world is a giant mechanism with gears and pulleys not visible to the eye, and I am just a figurine in a giant clock that has been wound up ages ago?*

John ate his eggs and left through a door he usually didn't take. Soot shook from the door as he opened it. If I'm part of a larger machine I'll change my pattern right now, he promised himself. As he went outside to be with the cows in the meadow, he thought that the day already seemed different than the rest. Later he realized he could have not been more right.

CHAPTER 4

The Great Bear

That evening John had eaten a light dinner and gone up to bed early. He had tried to keep as out of routine as possible. The thought that he could be part of an ancient machine would not give him rest. Within such a world there would be no meaning to his life. He would be like a gear turning on its axle until it wore out and then discarded like all things that wear out. In such a world there would be no escape.

As if in response to the shackles with which his ideas had imprisoned the universe, something quite out of the ordinary happened. John heard a bell ringing in the distance, Betsy's bell. That was not good. John opened the double doors to the cold air outside. He looked across the dark meadow toward the edge of the forest. The tree line seemed to stare back at him in silence, fog leaking from the trees down into the meadow below like foam from the mouth of a rabid dog.

The bell rang again and although he could not see Betsy, he knew the sound was coming from just inside the tree line. John ran downstairs to the barn hoping that Betsy was still in the stable and that her bell had just gotten caught in the bushes near the tree line as she was grazing. Betsy was nowhere to be found. John heaved open the heavy door and peered outside.

The meadow was covered with a low lying fog, lit by a full moon. A chill ran through John's spine—he had seen this before. He looked toward the other edge of the stable. Lying up against the far wall lay a four foot ax with a spear head on the top. At one time it had been a halberd, a spear length weapon used by Swiss mercenaries. John had cut it down to four feet so that he could chop wood with it. He picked up the shortened halberd and headed toward the door.

He peered outside, looking for movement. Again the bell rang. Without realizing what he was doing, he began walking out into the meadow. He felt like he was in the middle of a dream, but he knew what he was experiencing was no dream. He found himself slowly running through the meadow with the halberd in hand toward the sound of the bell. In the dream, he had felt as if his boots were glued to the ground. Now he could feel his bare feet squishing through the wet meadow floor, his legs plowing through the grass as if propelled by a will other than his own. His mind cleared as he came to the edge of the forest, looking up and down the tree line for the bear that haunted his dreams.

The wind blew and the bell rang again, now very close. Far down the tree line, several hundred yards away, he could see the fog swirling, moving toward the sound of the bell. John broke into a full sprint toward it. He was now twenty yards deep in the woods where the trees started to become too dense to pass through. The fog was thick and he needed to feel with hand and ax to keep from running into a tree. The wind blew again. He heard and then saw the bell. It hung from a bush close to the ground. Betsy was nowhere to be seen.

As John turned back to the house ready to sprint for the barn he heard a low growl. A patch of fur brushed by his arm, knocking the bell to the ground. He raised the halberd in front of him, ready to strike, but the fog was so thick his arms were but shadows drifting in the mist. His hair then began to blow across his face. As he looked out into the dark he could feel the fog swirling around him, but no sound could be heard.

He realized briefly that he was beyond fear and he felt overwhelmed with an intense loneliness. Would his death be the summation of a life lived in solitude and grief ending here in the wood alone and unloved? The meaninglessness of it all rushed over him like a flood and his soul cried out in anguish.

On cue, claws from the dark fog ripped across John's face, finding purchase in flesh and muscle. The first strike caught John off guard and he lowered the halberd. Teeth sunk into his right thigh and twirled him around as the animal began a macabre dance with John's body in the dark fog. Fur and claws now surrounded him, ripping and tearing at will. As the pain began to drift behind eyes blurred by blood, he heard the deafening roar of a huge bear. Mind, body, and soul reached their limit at that point, and John fell to the ground and remembered no more.

CHAPTER 5

Remembering

John awoke suddenly, his eyes matted shut with dried blood. The thought of the great bear was still fresh in his mind. As he began to sit up pain ran through him like a river through a narrow gorge. He lay in the stall next to Betsy, looking like a newborn calf covered in dried blood and straw. For how long he had lain in the straw he did not know but the ache in his muscles told him at least a full day. His mind shot back to the night of the bear. He had no clear recollection of anything other than a tempest of fog, teeth, claws, and fur. How he had survived was a miracle. How he had made it back to the stable was clear by the dried blood covering Betsy's back, a gruesome collage of deep reds and browns with John's full handprint on the side of her white neck. John reached up and touched the spot, still not believing that he was still alive. He looked down to his legs to assess the damage but no teeth marks could be found, only ripped flesh covered by a mortar of blood and ground straw.

John slowly pulled himself up off the ground using Betsy and the wall of her stall to brace himself. He felt stiff as if boards were nailed to his legs and as he moved toward the stairs he waddled more than he walked. Betsy stuck her head around the corner to watch as John headed toward the stairs. John stopped and looked up. The stairs could just as well have been a cliff. He looked down at his legs and then turned around to Betsy who was still staring at him and began to weep.

Several hours later, after the flood of despair had washed over and through him, he waddled over to the water trough and began to pull off the layers of blood and straw. As he ripped off layer after layer of blood, straw, and flesh his mind wandered elsewhere, not wanting to focus on the pain that enveloped him.

Images of himself as a young boy filled his mind. His mother rubbing his thick dark hair that curled and twisted like an unkempt vine left to its own direction. His mother had been a warm woman filled to the brim with love. Light seemed to seep out of her, brightening the soot covered kitchen. He could not remember a single moment of darkness in those years. But like so many women of that time, she died early. Of what, he was too young to understand, but he had never held to the notion that living in a kitchen full of smoke would not affect a person's health. It was a self made prison of soot that had kept her bound to her fate until death finally took her. Even as a boy John had hated that kitchen and had spent as little time in it as he could after his mother's passing.

A large piece of hay and blood ripped off his arm and John's mind returned to his bloodied body for a moment. He would need to be more careful or he would rip too deep and bleed out. A nervous laugh escaped him as he thought of himself being found dead by the water trough years down the road. What would the finder think? He began to peel off smaller pieces of the bloody mesh from his body and soon he was back into the rhythm of removing his outer shell of mortared blood.

His mind drifted to Becky in their early years. His memories lightened as he thought of picking flowers in the meadow for her as he watched the cows. Becky was always appreciative in the evening as he brought her in a bouquet, as if they were the first flowers she had ever received. He remembered her smile and the way her hair would blow in the breeze when they would walk in the field. They would stay up late in the evening and she would read to him. Together, for a moment, they were complete. But as time moved on, it became clear that they could not have children. The last year of her life she lingered in a sickly condition bound to the bed that John had built for them. John stopped going to the village that year, focusing all of his time on Becky, holding out the hope that she would recover, but she did not. When death finally took her he was broken to the core. It was then that he secluded himself in the work at the farm, and when that could not keep his mind off Becky he turned to immersing himself in the building of the cuckoo clocks, an obsession that soon spread to the entire house.

The life of light and love that he had shared with Becky had slowly evolved into a mechanical darkness, a darkness that threatened to consume him.

John's eyes opened wide and he screamed as he peeled off a piece of matted blood and straw that had encased his entire thigh. Fire ran through the leg and his breath left him for what seemed an eternity. Now panting, he looked beyond Betsy at a pile of straw lit by a sliver of light creeping in through a crack in the outer door.

Was this to be the sum of his life? John looked down at himself and in that moment decided he was not going to go quietly into the night. Dragging himself up to the water trough, he grabbed onto Betsy's side and heaved his body into the trough, fully submerging himself in the water. What was left of the blood and straw began to break off and float to the surface. When he climbed out he could move with great pain, but now the pain seemed like a distant thought. Slowly making his way to the outer door he opened it wide, flooding the stable with light. Where this new resolve would lead him he did not know, but wherever it led him, he would no longer be confined to the dark.

CHAPTER 6

Letting Some Light In

Over the next several days John nursed his wounds and spent most of his time cutting windows into his huge house. Light crept into places that had never before seen the sun. The last room to be opened up was the kitchen. John placed an especially large window in the soot filled crypt of his childhood. The old floorboards in the kitchen winced at the bright intrusion. The life sized effigy of Becky was also dismantled, cleaned and placed in a corner in the stable to watch over the cows. When John was done he had made nearly the entire west wall of the house into windows. The black that had enveloped the great fire pit of the kitchen was now a thousand shades of grey harmoniously darting in and out of the stone circle. The wind whipped through the room pulling soot off the metal top of the pit, which then shimmered in the sunlight like water in a fast moving brook racing in one direction and then the next.

Later that day John sat in the kitchen looking out the great window over the meadow. Spring flowers were now filling the field, and with John's help now filled the kitchen, placed haphazardly in any glass or container he could find. When he ran out of containers he took to laying them on the tables and floor. Broad strokes of red and orange now filled the once dark room. The color almost sang out to John, so moved was he by the sight. The breeze had a cool clean fragrance to it and John's heart lightened for a moment, but it was not enough. John looked around him and for the first time since Becky had died he realized that he was alone. It was an odd thing to look out at the meadow dancing and swaying in the wind like an ocean of colored light, moving in wave after wave as the grass and the flowers bowed to the will of the wind.

It seemed hollow watching this spectacle alone, but Becky, the one he had shared all things with, was gone. In his moment of reflection a thought crept into his mind, that of a small child running through the tall grass of the meadow. His mind traced the imaginary path meandering over hill and over rock in a playful course only a child could follow. To find another wife was not conceivable, but children were a different matter. The same sickness that had taken his Becky had also left many children orphaned in the village. Some had been shipped off to relatives far away, but not all. A week ago the thought of bringing children out to the farm would have seemed absurd, but that was before he had passed through the tunnel of death and popped out the other end still alive. Now anything seemed possible. Even hope seemed possible, a luxury that he had not indulged in for years.

The gears in his mind began to spin as he brought to mind the priest in the village. He would go to the village tomorrow and talk to the priest about orphans in the area. He would build a family, as he had built the mechanical house. A cool breeze swept through the open window and he knew that he would need to put shutters over the new cut windows. Even in the spring the nights were cold and damp, and the kitchen fire could only heat a closed house. His eyes drifted toward the walls where the mechanism that had moved Becky about the kitchen was housed. In his mind he imagined gears and belts operating shutters throughout the house.

As he rose to head upstairs to prepare a more detailed plan he caught some movement in the trees at the edge of the forest from the corner of his eye. His attention soon focused on the spot at the forest's edge where his flesh had been torn. A chill ran through him but soon left as there was much work to be done. He had a life to rebuild. He watched as the sun set over the meadow and the ocean of color was covered with the greys of twilight. Before he headed upstairs to put his plans to action he looked back one more time at the forest's edge. He saw nothing but felt the weight of eyes watching him as he went upstairs to the workshop.

CHAPTER 7

The Following Morning

The road to the village amounted to nothing more than two ruts in the earth overgrown with weeds. John was the only one to have reason to be on the road and it had now been over two years since his last trip to the village. Behind him he pulled a cart full of cuckoo clocks for sale at the market. Small red posies lined the edges of his path like a blood trail leading him toward the steeple that marked the edge of town. The air was fresh and the sun was bright. Perspiration rolled off his brow and his back ached from pulling the cart. Years back he had a horse to do this work but he had died during the solitude of the last two years and up to now John had not given a thought to replacing him. John looked over his shoulder at the cart full of clocks, two full years of work. He would either sell the cart or buy a horse. The road to the village was mostly downhill and he had no intention of hauling the cart back to the farm on his own.

It was midday when he arrived at the church in the village. The village roads were narrow, some so much so that only a single cart would fit through and sometimes even that would be tight. The church sat on top of a hill, not high enough to see the tile roofs on top of all the buildings, but tall enough to see the cobblestone streets slowly slope off toward the brook that ran through the town. Colorful signs stuck out from the light stone buildings marking the various shops, most of which had been in place for more than a hundred years. It was now near midday and the streets were filled with men dressed much like John in dark trousers and vests with bright white shirts underneath. The ladies wore dresses that dropped to their feet, many wearing hats adorned with large red or black balls signifying if they were married or looking. Not unlike the signs on the stores, John thought with a chuckle.

An orange sign halfway down the main road next to the bakery caught his eye. It was a general store run by a childhood friend of his, Helmut, and John knew Helmut would find a place for his clocks in the store. John's stomach rumbled at the smell of the fragrant breads inside the bakery. He looked back up at the church and saw Aeneas talking to a man near the front door of the church. His mind focused back in on the reason he had made this journey in the first place. Father Aeneas would know if there were orphans in the town that were in need of a home. It was here where his search would begin. The man that Aeneas was talking to left and John made his way up the stairs to the large wooden doors at the front of the church.

Aeneas looked down and smiled as he saw John walking toward him. He wore a thick brown woolen robe tied by a simple rope. In his earlier years he had been a Franciscan monk spending most of his time secluded in the forest, and he was one of the few men alive that had ventured down the forest paths into areas where the sun no longer shone. The people said it had changed him but he spoke little of it himself. When the village priest had died thirty years ago he had just shown up and taken on the duties of the priest. Occasionally Father would be seen wandering out into the woods wearing only his robe and a walking stick and be gone for days.

"John, you would have made a fine horse," Father said, smiling and waving him over.

John's face reddened as he shrugged his shoulders.

"It has been a long time since you have been in town, John. What brings you in today?" As John moved in closer, Father could see the bruises and partially healed cuts on John's face. His smile turned more somber as he brought his hand up to rub his beard as if deep in thought.

"It was a bear at the west end of the wood." John turned and waved his hand toward the forest behind him.

"You live close to the forest, John." He then hushed his voice. "There are many things in the forest. Some of them very dangerous." He then leaned in closer, his voice now only a whisper. "Did you actually see the great bear?"

John shook his head. "The fog was thick. But I remember hearing the roar." John then looked down at his arms still crisscrossed with fresh healing wounds. "I was as close as I will ever want to be."

"It's a tricky business being in the thick fog of the forest." The Father's hand reached out to John's. "Sometimes things are not as they seem."

John felt strangely comforted by Father's firm grip. His hands were nearly half the size of John's, but they were so strong he felt as if his own hands were those of a child who was being consoled by his real father. With his arm reached out John could see many scars on Father's arm, some still fresh from within the last two weeks, cutting through others that were years old. As John looked closer it was hard to find a portion that was not scarred heavily. "You have seen the great bear?"

"Yes John, I have. But now is not the time to talk of it." Father Aeneas began leading John down the stairs toward the cart full of clocks. "You came to town for other business. Let me walk with you to the shop and we can share lunch." The Father grabbed one handle of the cart and John the other and the two began making their way farther into town. "I have not seen you since the death of Becky, John. Have you been up at the farm alone all this time?"

John looked over to Father Aeneas and nodded. "I did not realize how lonely I had been until after the bear attack." Sadness filled John's heart. "Becky and I were never able to have children." A tear welled in John's eye. "It was a dream of hers."

"It sounds like you could use some company, John."

The cart was heavy but Father Aeneas carried most of the load, which surprised John. He stood almost two feet shorter than John and had at least thirty years on him. As the two men reached the shop the smell of fresh bakery bread grew more enticing. They began to unload the clocks.

"After we have all the clocks in the shop you can finish your business with Helmut and I will go next door and get us some bread and cheese for lunch. I will meet you outside on the bench."

CHAPTER 8

The Hunt

Franz looked down a narrow alley in the village. His hunters were nowhere in sight. He looked tall for an eight year old, but much of the height came from the wild bush of curly blond hair that swayed to and fro when he walked. Loose clothing given to him by Father Aeneas, now tattered, covered his wiry body. The Father had taught him how to move silently in the alleys and in the forest, blending in the shadows and corners on the path. He leapt more than he ran as he moved from shadow to shadow like a squirrel leaping from branch to branch. The dried mud in his hair blended in with the stone buildings in the background providing a natural camouflage. His brother and sister who hunted him were good, but he would win the game today. Franz stopped for a moment, tucking himself in behind a garbage pail and caught his breath as he looked down the alley toward the main street.

At the end of the alley he saw Father Aeneas and a man larger than he had ever seen pulling a cart down the street. Father Aeneas did not go into town very often, and thus, this was a curious event that demanded further investigation. Franz looked behind him on the rooftops. He had not been spotted yet. If he went onto the main street he would lose his cover, but that was a chance he would have to take. Franz slowly made his way down to where the alley met the street to take a closer look.

* * * * *

Max crouched down on a rooftop three blocks away. Max was fourteen years old and stood nearly six feet tall. He wore rags similar to those that

21

covered Franz. His arms and legs flowed with well-toned muscles, enough to hold his own in a fight but not so much as to slow him down in a run. He and his twin sister had been hunting Franz all morning but had seen nothing. The sky was blue and even though it was early in the spring, the sun was growing hot in the midday.

A bead of sweat rolled down his nose and as he scanned the village he thought back at their first meeting with Father Aeneas. Their parents had died from the sickness that had devastated the village. Their family was poor and they had no other family. There were men in front of a dark room reading through a will when a man in a brown robe stepped out of a shadow in the corner and ruffled his hands through the children's hair as he made his way to the men. They seemed as surprised to see him as the children. After a short discussion Father returned to the children, knelt down, and brought them into his arms, telling them they would stay with him from that point on. The change had been difficult at first, as Father had a strange habit of roaming in the forest, but over time they had come to enjoy the jaunts into the woods as much as Father did. Father Aeneas had taught Max and Mary the bow, but allowed them to only kill what they would later eat. Most of what they shot at were small tags he would place on the trees that they passed in the forest. They were taught to always hunt as a pair, he and Mary. But that seemed only natural as he and Mary had always done everything together.

Max returned to the moment and saw Mary moving gracefully down one of the alleyways weaving between barrels like a dear in the forest would move through heavy brush. Like Max, she had long black hair, but unlike Max, she let it flow freely as opposed to being tied up in the back. Mary was built similar to Max, just one size smaller. Even though their clothes all came from the same rag bin, she presented herself with a more refined look. There were no torn edges to her dress, and the blues in her blouse complemented the sea grey of her eyes.

Mary looked up and saw Max nod his head toward the main street. Mary and Max seldom needed to speak when they were on the hunt, a nod here and a twitch there was all that was needed. It was almost as if they knew the mind of the other as they flowed through the forest and the village. Mary wondered why Max was moving her toward the main street. Franz would never go there. There was no place to hide.

CHAPTER 9

Introductions

John came out from the shop and saw that Father Aeneas had already found a seat in front of the bakery.

"I don't want to alarm you, John, but we are being watched." Father Aeneas smiled and tilted his head toward a barrel at the edge of an alleyway.

At first John thought he was looking at a small bush coming out of the top of the barrel, but then the bush shifted and he could make out the outline of a young boy. John smiled and lifted up his bread and waved the boy over. At first there was no response, but then John pointed to the cheese. This proved enough to uproot the bush and Franz bounded over and sat in between the two men. John reached down and pulled back the hair so he could see the boy's eyes, blue like the sky. "I am John." John smiled and handed Franz a piece of cheese wrapped in bread.

Franz took it and smiled and then began to devour his unexpected meal. He was most certainly spotted by Max by now, but that did not matter. No prize at the end of the day would compare to warm bread and cheese. He smiled. Let them watch me eat. Franz looked up and saw Max on the rooftop across the street, his hands on his hips, looking down on him. Franz waved his bread at him. Nothing else needed to be said.

"This young man is one of three children I have been taking care of for the past three years, John." Father Aeneas ran his hand through the boy's hair. "His name is Franz."

The boy looked up and nodded as if to affirm the truth of the matter.

"I have a favor to ask you, John." The Father picked up Franz and put him on his knee. "The children have been living cooped up in the church these last three years. Children need space to roam and play. Take them to the farm with you for the summer. A little work would do them good."

John smiled so broad he thought his heart would burst. He reached his hand out to Franz, who looked up at the great hairy man. A small hand emerged from the golden bush of hair and landed on John's giant palm. Their eyes met, not knowing what to expect.

"So where are your hunters, Franz?" John asked, smiling as he looked down at the tiny hand in his palm.

Franz blushed as he motioned behind John. John turned and found the twins watching him with some concern.

John stood as he took in the twins. They gave away nothing in their eyes, waiting for him to make the first move, and so he did.

"My name is John, son of Hans. I have been living in the farm west of town alone for three years. Father Aeneas has volunteered your services for the summer and the company would do me good. I would be honored to have you return to my farm with me tonight if that would be acceptable to you." John stood now with only a smile.

Max and Mary looked at Father Aeneas and he nodded and smiled. The twins looked at each other and nodded, and Max extended his hand to John. "We will join you for the summer and do what we can to help at your farm."

John looked at the children in their rags and then at the bag of silver that he had received for the clocks he traded earlier in the day. "It would seem that it has been some time since you have had properly fitting clothes." John grabbed the bag of silver and led the children down the street to the tailor who was also a childhood friend of his. There he left some silver with Father and led Mary to a neighboring dress shop.

Mary had passed the shop many times looking in the window at the many dresses adorned with embroidered flowers and birds. She had imagined herself wearing all of them, but had not dared of dreaming of owning any of them. John took her into the shop and the shop keeper stepped back for a moment when he saw Mary and the rags that she wore. John hefted the bag of silver on the counter top, which lightened the mood in the room, and Mary began trying on the many dresses that she had only dreamed of wearing.

The five met up at the church later that afternoon carrying several bags of clothes and the two bows that Father Aeneas had given them. Franz was too young for a bow, but Father had not left him defenseless. Around his waist he wore a belt with several throwing knives, a detail that John had not yet noticed. The children had no other belongings.

* * * * *

"You had better get going, John, if you are to make the farm before nightfall." Father Aeneas gave each of the children a kiss and a hug and sent them off with John. He waved as they passed his line of sight.

It was a curious thing that he had been forbidden to tell them anything of the wolves and the great bear. It would have seemed to him to be useful information. But he had moved beyond questioning the path a long time ago. He went inside the church carrying the remainder of the silver which John had given for the poor. All he had said of the matter was that he had everything he needed at the farm and had no need of silver.

Father placed the silver in a safe place and grabbed a broad-edged sword from a hidden opening in the wall. He headed out the back of the church and into the forest. The wolves would be out tonight and there was much work to be done.

CHAPTER 10

Pulleys and Ropes

Max tensed as he awoke to a subtle ticking sound within the wall. He imagined a mouse running within the wall and slid out of bed to chase the sound. Mary and Franz still lay asleep next to him in John's old bed. As he slid his boots on, he reached back and rubbed his neck. He had grown accustomed to sleeping on a hard bunk in the rectory. He could get used to a real bed. He lifted his head as the noise started up again, this time in the ceiling, making its way across the bedroom toward the kitchen. Careful not to wake the others, he crept forward toward the door. What he saw after he opened it he could not have imagined.

"Come in and close the door so that you don't wake the others." John motioned him in with his hand.

John was sitting at the table with a plate full of ham. Behind John the world was a blur of rope and pulley and mechanical arms busily tending to their business. Max heard a clunk in the corner and saw an egg emerge from a hole in the wall. It rolled down a metal chute onto what looked like a large spoon levered on the table with a spring at its base. Without warning a latch pulled away and the spoon released, propelling the egg on its maiden voyage, almost the full length of the kitchen, into a wire funnel, and still in one piece followed the hole in the funnel into a frying pan that had just been set there by a mechanical arm that emerged from the wall. Bellows roared on the side and the fire in the pit in the middle of the kitchen came to life. John motioned Max to sit down and then placed a plate in front of him over an X that had been carved into the table. Without delay a three-egg omelet flipped through the air and flopped onto the plate, half sliding off. John reached over with his fork and centered the omelet on the plate.

"Still working on that part." John stared down at the plate as if in deep thought. "Still a little shell in the middle. It's a work in progress." John turned his attention back to his ham as an omelet came flying onto his plate, bounced off the ham, and toppled several feet down the table. John reached over with his fork and playfully flipped the eggs back onto his plate and gestured to Max to go ahead and eat.

"Did you create all of this?" Max looked around him as mechanical gadgets continued to tend to their designed function.

"I have been busy these last several years." John's face nearly burst with pride. "Would you like to see how it all works?"

After they ate John led Max to a door in the back of the kitchen and opened it. The smell of oiled rope and metal filled the room. The two walked in carefully as there were many holes in the floor where ropes or gears made their way down to do their work in the lower levels. Stepping around a slowly turning gear that stood nearly as tall as Max, John went toward the center of the machine, his own invention. There in the middle of the room stood a giant coiled spring that rose through the ceiling like the trunk of a great tree into the next floor. It shined of polished metal, even in the dim light of the machine room. It quivered ever so slightly as it very slowly unwound, driving the large gear to its side. Off that gear many smaller gears fed, in turn driving a whole chain of gears that directed the inner workings of the house. It seemed to Max that he was in a beehive with motion all around him or perhaps in a pit of snakes as greased and oiled ropes slithered up and down the outer walls. As Max saw the ropes running up and down the walls his eyes fell to his own body.

John saw Max looking down at his hand moving his fingers in and out as if they were run by gears and pulleys on the inside. "It is a curious thought." John looked down at his own hand, as he had done before, moving his fingers as Max did. "I have been cut deep and have never seen any gears in my body, no pulleys or levers directing their action. And yet our motion is so similar to the machine that it must be the same at some level. Perhaps the gears and ropes are so small that our eyes cannot make them out but I am convinced they exist. I have created this machine, but it is only a crude replica of the machine that is the world. Our arms and legs and hands and feet, as elegant as they are, are only the next gear down in the infinite line of gears in the greater machine that we call the world."

Max furrowed his brows as he still looked down at his fingers moving in and out. "But I choose to move my finger." Max then held his hand still. "And I choose not to move my finger. How do I fit into your machine?"

John smiled and put his arm around Max as he led him to the upper level of the house. "I have not fully worked that one out yet."

As they entered the upper level Max took in the aroma of hay and pine shavings from the workshop. In the background he saw the bulk of the house's machinery. Max had a natural curiosity that kept his mind sharp and his eyes keen on details. In their travels in the forest with Father Aeneas, Max was always asking questions about trees and shrubs. There were berries good for eating and herbs that could be used for healing a wound. Max had also paid close attention to the tracks on the trail. Father would say little of the wolf track that they occasionally saw. Max thought it odd that even though some of the tracks were fresh, they never saw a wolf when they were out. Some of the tracks would end abruptly in the trail with nothing to explain their sudden disappearance other than a slight tinge of purple in the soil. The priest would say little of these areas, mostly talking about the mystery of the forest, and soon they would be talking about the many uses of cherry pits.

Max's eyes drifted over to John. To build such a machine he had to be a very smart man. He would take John out onto the trails and see what he could make of these mysteries. Everything run by tiny machines. The thought was intriguing, hard to let go of … like the wolf tracks. Max looked back down at his hand and moved his fingers one by one. In many ways the thoughts were like the paths in the forest; if he followed them long enough and deep enough he could not predict where he would end up. He and John spent over an hour following gears to ropes to pulleys until Max understood how the entire apparatus worked. When they returned to the kitchen Mary and Franz were already sitting at the table. Max saw John move a lever as he entered the room and soon the eggs started to roll again.

John sat down with the children and moved the plates over the X's on the table. "Father Aeneas said he had trained you with the bow." An omelet flew onto the plate in front of Franz, who pushed his hair back to see the rest of the show. "This morning we will see how good you are."

John pushed a bowl of bread and plate of butter across the table. "There is a bear that lives in the woods, who comes and goes in the fog of the night hunting at the edge of the forest. When we are good enough we will hunt him. Until then no one goes into the forest without me."

Mary smiled. She wondered whether Father had told John how much time they had spent in the forest. "Thank you for taking us in for the summer."

Franz looked up and nodded. His mouth and hair were full of food.

"What can we do to help out with the farm?" Mary reached over and picked a piece of egg out of Franz's hair. "We have never lived at a farm before."

As if on cue, the shutters on the kitchen's new window opened, letting the morning sun soak into the room. "Much of the house takes care of itself, but there are still chores to be done outside. Let's eat first, and then I'll show you what they are."

CHAPTER 11

Target Practice

After they finished their breakfast John showed Max and Franz how to milk the cows and took Mary out to the garden plot. Mary had never planted things in the past. Before their parents had died she had spent most of her days with mother helping with chores around the house, but once they were gone there was no home to care for. Hours spent playing in the house and field were gradually replaced by hunting with Max. At first she had no interest in going into the forest with the boys, but Father Aeneas had made every trip into the woods a game and she was very good at games. Each day was a new adventure. Before she knew what had happened she was running the trails with Max, two people with one mind moving in tandem, always knowing where the other would be next. She tried not to think of the past, only moving forward. Her only real concern was Franz, who was still young enough to need more than the hunt. Her mind drifted back to the dirt as she tilled a portion of the soil in front of her with her hands. The soil was cool and the grit of the dirt felt good as it rubbed on her skin.

* * * * *

Later that day John assembled the children on the far side of the house where he had erected a target on a mound of hay. The twins' bows and two quivers of arrows lay beside it. John pointed to a mound thirty yards out and motioned the children out for their first target practice. Max and Mary took their positions, looked at each other, smiled, and nodded. Quickly they both drew an arrow and let loose simultaneously. Both arrows found their mark in the middle of the target. They then took off from the mound, flanking the target both left and right. Arrows came in rapid fire, from which twin John lost track. The target's center was filled with arrows.

John sat there dumfounded with his mouth hanging open, looking over to Franz, who was sitting next to him. Franz looked up, pulled his hair back, smiled, and shrugged his shoulders as if nothing more need be said. Franz then bounded up and over to the mound. He had no bow, for he was too small. He then began to run and leap in a zigzag motion toward the target. From his belt he pulled one small throwing knife after the next. Each found their mark around the arrows in the target. He finished his run in front of the target, turned toward John, and put his hands on his hips as if awaiting applause.

John jumped up and ran to Franz and put him up on his shoulder. Franz smiled, holding tight to John's massive head. John then congratulated the twins. "Perhaps we will be hunting for the bear sooner than I thought." John smiled as he helped pull arrows out of the target. It promises to be an interesting summer, he thought.

CHAPTER 12

Several Months Later

Franz leapt down the trail only yards in front of John. It was midsummer and the forest was filled with the songs of birds and the chatter of insects. It had rained just last night and the air hung heavy with the smell of pine. The paths in the forest were wide, ten yards at their narrowest.

Franz looked ahead at Max and Mary disappearing around a corner, one on the left, one on the right, always ready to flank whatever they might find on the path. He lunged toward a sapling oak and felt the mark he had carved into it several weeks prior. The paths crisscrossed and the markings on the trees were the only way they would find their way back to the farm this far into the forest. There were more fresh wolf trails the deeper they went in, but they had still not seen a single wolf.

Franz looked back at John, who was too far back for comfort. "Hurry, father, Max and Mary are already out of sight." Franz lowered his head and whipped his hair above his eyes, providing a clear view of John for a moment.

John smiled and picked up his pace. Franz had started calling him "Father John" their first week together. He had tried to explain he was not a priest like Father Aeneas, but the father had stuck. The twins still called him John. At first they did not know what to make of the tightening bond between John and Franz, but once Mary seemed comfortable with it Max just went along.

John sped around the corner of the path and found Max and Mary crouched with bows drawn looking down a fork in the path. Behind them was the body of a wolf, his head a few yards ahead. The dirt around the body had a purple hue, brighter than the stains they had found on other paths. The body of the wolf was still warm, but no blood flowed from the neck.

Franz ran up next to John as John picked up the wolf's head. "It was a sharp blade … one blow," he ventured.

John looked down at Franz, who was now leaning into his leg. "We are not alone."

Mary looked back. "There are no tracks other than the wolf's."

Max nodded. "Whoever this hunter is, he moves without being seen on the trail … like a ghost."

John waved his halberd, signaling the children to follow him back the way they had come. "Ghost or no ghost, we will head home. Perhaps we should not have ventured so deep into the forest."

No one said a word for the next several hours as they quickly made their way back to the forest's edge. It was a quiet supper that night. As twilight passed into darkness John grabbed a blanket and headed out to the meadow as he often did in the summer to look up to the stars and calm his mind. It was not long before Franz and the twins came to join him. The evening was cool and the stars were bright like arrows of light raining down from the heavens and piercing into the ground.

"I look at the stars and see tiny gears in a clock moving a great machine in the sky." Max smiled, propping his head up behind folded arms. "With each star being pulled along the sky by levers in the dark night."

John smiled and nodded. He and Max had spent long nights talking of clocks and gears. It was hard not to let the conversation drift into speculation. "If the world is a machine I should like to know how to move the lever to control it."

A hawk flew across the night sky, silhouetted by the stars behind. Franz rolied his eyes as he always did whenever John and Max talked of gears and he snuggled closer to John trying to stay warm. "I love the stars. They seem alive in the sky as they watch us. I wonder what a star might think."

Mary smiled. "Perhaps they would think that we are as beautiful as they are, reaching out at us as they lie on their blanket." Mary reached out as if to pluck a star from the sky.

"Perhaps the lever to control the sky is under here." John reached under Franz and began to tickle him, and he and the children laughed into the night.

CHAPTER 13

The Family

John stood in the middle of the meadow with the moon at his back. At the tree line he could see the great bear moving along the edge of the trees. The moonlight reflected off its dark brown fur shimmering like a regal robe. John reached down for his knife but instead found a cuckoo clock in his hand. The bear turned toward him and not so much looked at him but through him. John hid himself with his arm. He was exposed. Secrets hidden deep, fears long since forgotten were laid out in the open. Sweat dripped from his brow as he stood fully clothed and yet naked in the meadow.

With a start he woke up, his pillow wet with perspiration. The dreams of the bear that had haunted him through the winter had returned as the summer waned to an end. It was time to bring the children back to Father Aeneas. John could not bear the thought of separation. He looked over at Franz curled up in the corner of his bed. They had become almost inseparable over the last months. He, too, had started to dream of the bear. He told John of running with the bear in the forest in the heat of the day. John had tried to make something of the dreams, but Franz did not worry over them.

John put on his boots and headed over to the workbenches to pack up the cuckoo clocks he and the children had made together. As he wrapped them for the trip he noted that the dark blues and greens had been replaced with bright yellows and reds on the clocks. Franz liked the brighter colors and now that John thought of it, they had grown on him, too. Later that afternoon John and the children made their way back to the village. John carried most of the clocks in a sack over one shoulder, with Franz sitting on the other. Mary looked ahead at the two and tears filled her eyes. They had all grown close over the summer, but Franz most of all. She could not recall a moment over that last week that she did not see them together, as if Franz could sense the impending separation.

It was mid afternoon when they reached the church. The front door was open and dust lay on the altar. Mary ran a finger across the stone. "It is unlike Father Aeneas not to keep things clean."

Max made a quick sweep of the church and rectory with no sign of life. "He's been gone for a while." Max walked back with a plate of moldy bread. "And it looks like he left in a hurry."

John had the children stay at the church and he went down to sell the clocks and find out where the priest had gone. He came back an hour later with a bag full of bread and pastries.

"He disappeared the same day we left. No one has seen him since." Not knowing what else to do, John took out a piece of bread and passed it around.

Everyone looked at everyone, not wanting to be the first one to speak. Franz broke the silence. "Well, I guess we should head back to the farm before it gets dark." With that the four headed out of church back to the farm. Little was said on the way back, but that afternoon the four became a family.

CHAPTER 14

The Splitter

It was now Midwinter's Eve and still no word from Father Aeneas. They still made excursions into the forest paths, but not as deep as they had the day they found the wolf. The snow was heavy outside the house and most of their days were spent either making clocks or working on the house. John looked over at Franz and Mary painting small trees and birds. He had just spent several hours with Franz carving those very same birds. Max waited for him down in the machine room. He had tried to get Franz interested in the mechanics of the house but he had no interest. Those hours in the "gear room" as Franz would put it were the only hours the two were separated.

"It's about time you made it down." Max was covered in grease from head to toe. Gears lay strewn over the floor. The great spring that drove the machine of the house was partly unwound and quivered like an animal ready to attack.

"It looks like you have been doing fine without me, Max." John took hold of the great spring and pulled slightly sending a spiraling wave through the coiled monstrosity. "We will need to add at least twenty feet of coil to run the wood splitter out back."

Max nodded. It was a huge device with several ax blades and a trough to carry the split wood into the house. Max enjoyed splitting wood by ax but he had been the one who designed the splitter. At the time it seemed a natural expansion of the machine. It was not the only handiwork the two had been up to over the winter. Nearly every function of the house now ran by gear, lever, and rope. The only area of the house that remained free of the machine's rule was the workshop above. They had considered creating a device that could make the clocks but when they arrived with a burlap bag full of gears and rope they were met with the disapproving stare of Franz and Mary. That was as close as the machine's grasp came to that hallowed ground. There the line had been drawn and for the time being would have to be respected. It was an odd thing adding extensions on the machine. Max enjoyed working with his hands on the clocks as much as Mary and Franz, but it only seemed natural to mechanize it. Then they would be free to spend their time in other ways. Max looked back at the great spring. "The last piece of metal to be added is over there."

John looked over to the corner. He hauled up the metal and held it in place as Max fastened it to the great spring and together they rewound the spring and set it. John went upstairs to the open window and jumped out to the rope, pulling up the frozen cow counterweight. For the first try he only went halfway down to the level of the machine room and entered a window that he and Max had cut to allow for a half winding of the machine. Cold air flooded the room, frosting the metal gears and spring as he entered. He and Max stood back as they watched the spring tighten and then slowly turn the great gear that drove all other gears.

"Here it goes." Max held his breath and pulled the lever that connected the wood splitter outside. They stood silent as they listened for any activity that could confirm their success. A boom and a clunk could be barely heard, muffled by the falling snow outside. John and Max ran upstairs to watch as a piece of split wood fell through a trap door high up on the wall and onto a pile of wood near the pile that fed the fire in the kitchen below.

If pride could have been converted to heat, John was pretty sure the glow from the two engineers could have heated the house that night without the help of the fire below. Much of the remainder of the day was spent reconnecting the gears that attached the rest of the house back to the machine. John went to sleep late that night smelling of oil that permeated his flesh … the dark perfume of the machine.

CHAPTER 15

Rusty Dreams

That night, as John closed his eyes, the reality of this world gave way to the realm of his dreams. He stood in the middle of the snow filled meadow that glowed from the moon above. He scanned the tree line for the bear but he was not to be found. He tried to pick up his leg but it would not move, only making a creaking sound of rusted metal on metal.

John looked down and saw that his torso and legs had been replaced with mechanical counterparts of rusted gears and ratchets near each joint. He had one metal arm that still moved and he waved the mechanical hand in front of his face. Behind the rusted exterior he could see tiny moving parts like bees swarming on a honeycomb. Many nights he had mused over the inner workings of his own body, imagining a mechanical device, but now seeing it with his own eyes in the dream, he was horrified as he moved each finger in sequence. Turning his hand over, he exposed the only polished surface on his body and in the moonlight saw his reflection on the cold metal plate. At first he thought the mechanical face was just a picture until he furled his eyebrows and saw the corresponding movement in the mirror. John's breath deepened and quickened as panic filled his metal body. Without thought he took his one free arm and began tearing metal from his body, like a man ripping burning clothing from his flesh. Soon the pristine white of the snow was littered with the rust orange wreckage of his metal body. Gears and metal plates stuck out of the snow haphazardly like tombstones in an unkempt cemetery.

John woke up in a deep oily sweat. He grabbed his body and then his face, not yet convinced that his flesh had returned. The dreams were becoming more real as the winter wore on, but this was the first that the bear had not appeared. John looked around at the gear and rope that lined the walls of the room. They were dark and made him feel dirty. He loved and yet now hated the machine that he lived in, but in his heart he knew there was no escape. Day after day it was absorbing him, and now Max. He would need to do something, but what he did not know. As he drifted back to sleep his mind tore the machine down and at the same time mended the damage. If it were left to him he would never be free.

CHAPTER 16

One Log Too Many

That morning Max and Mary woke early as they had done every morning that winter to hunt the shallow trail of the forest. Wild game had returned to the trails near the farm and hunting had been good the last several weeks. With bows in hand they headed toward the upper floor. The cold wind bit as they opened the doors. It was still dark out but the moon shone bright on the snow. It would be day soon. They smiled and lunged out toward the rope that wound the new spring in the house. Neither was heavy enough alone to bring down the rope, but they could do it together. As they descended they met the frozen cow halfway down as it took its place near the peak of the house. They looked back as they made their way through the snow toward the forest and saw smoke coming up from the chimney. The machine was wound. Franz and John would awake to a warm house. The two disappeared into the forest following wood grouse tracks that were fresh from last night.

As the new spring unwound in the house the gears and levers faithfully went about their chores. The new wood splitter out back had plenty of wood and split log after log, which piled up near the trap door above the kitchen. With the next opening of the trap door three times too many logs fell into the kitchen fire pit.

The bellows blew and the fire roared with joy. Now overfed, the fire licked the ceiling boards with yellow and orange flame. Smoke soon filled the second floor of the house. At daybreak the window shutters in the kitchen opened as they were designed and the house took a deep breath in as cool air raced toward the fire. A quick exhale of roaring flame followed and smoke began to fill the upper level of the house where John and Franz still slept.

Franz was the first of the two to wake. The smoke was a thick veil in the dark room and Franz choked as he leapt from the bed. He looked back for John feeling on the blankets but he was already disoriented and felt nothing but an empty bed. It was time for the window shutters on the upper level to open and again the house took a deep breath. For a moment enough of the smoke cleared that Franz could see the fire roaring near the back side of the house where the hay was kept, cutting off his ground floor exit. The fire was racing toward him and he saw only one escape, the ladder that led to a trap door at the peak of the thatched roof. He had played on the ladder nearly every day in the summer and that escape route was the first thought that came to mind. He had no plan once on the rooftop.

The machine room was now a furnace of fire and oil and red hot metal. The great spring that was the lifeblood of the house was not designed for such temperatures and it expanded and warped until all restraint was lost. The spring of coiled metal shuddered and then with an explosion uncoiled, tearing out the charred walls of the second floor.

John sat up straight at the sound of the explosion, the smoke now cleared by great holes of fire in the thatch roof and the walls around him. His mind raced as he saw his home consumed with flame and then the thought of Franz filled his mind, and he looked down on the bed and saw nothing. He jumped to his feet and looked toward the workbenches but saw nothing. It was then that he felt the coolness of snow on his face. He looked up and saw the trap door to the thatch roof open and knew in a moment where Franz had disappeared to and what was now required.

John ran to the open doors and grabbed the rope that Max and Mary had pulled down only an hour before. He held tight and pulled the rope up the ladder with him, flames licking both the rope and the ladder. John raced up the ladder and like a wick to a candle the fire lit his oil laden body aflame. John poked his head though the snow at the rooftop, now fully ablaze. Sitting there near the opening was Franz, who pulled back at first at the sight of the furry man on fire. Not waiting a moment he scooped Franz up with an armful of snow to insulate him from the flame that engulfed him and began running down the steep thatch roof with Franz in one hand and the rope in the other. When the rope ran out and pulled tight he jumped into the open air and swung across the front of the house. The thatch where they had just been standing burst into flame. At the upper end of the arc of their swing the rope broke with fire still eating at the frayed edge. If someone was watching from the forest they would have seen a fire ball of a man sailing through the air and plugging into a snow bank twenty yards from the house.

Burned from head to toe, John jumped out of the snow at the sound of an explosion as barrels full of grain dust exploded in the manger. The cows ran out of the burning building before the great structure collapsed in on itself. Bright hot gears and half melted pieces of metal rained down all around them. John grabbed Franz and running on mindless adrenaline he headed for the tree line. He plowed through the snow like a bull through a wheat field not yet feeling any of the pain from the charred flesh that now covered his body. There ahead was the very spot that he had been mauled last spring. He burst through the first line of trees and then collapsed on a bed of pine needles, throwing Franz several yards ahead into a snowy bush. What was left of his burnt clothes had fallen off on the run through the snowy meadow. His blackened body now lay charred on the bloodied forest floor, a battlefield of one lone rebel. Beaten down by a lifelong war with his master, John now lay in ruin.

* * * * *

Franz pulled himself out of the bush and rushed to John only to find his adopted father covered in blood and charred flesh on the ground. The grim sight led him to back up several feet into a warm wet nose. Hot breath poured over Franz as he spun around to find the great bear watching him and John. Franz jumped back and climbed up onto John's back, pulling two knives from his belt. His toes sunk into John's seared flesh as he readied himself for the charge.

John was the only father Franz had ever known and he swore to himself he would not give him up to the bear. The great bear roared, blowing back Franz's hair, and the small warrior leaned into the roar with blades held tight ready to make his last stand. Franz met the gaze of the bear and was filled with a wonderful terror.

CHAPTER 17

Alone In the Snow

"How much farther to the farm?" Max trudged through the snow with three wood grouse slung over his back. The canopy over the path was dense, but not dense enough to keep the storm above from invading the forest. Winter's cold breath poured through the trees above, swirling snow through the tender rafters that held the forest's roof intact. Dead leaves still clung tight to the oaks high above mingled with the towering pines allowing only a veiled promise of light from the grey sky.

"We should be getting close to the forest's edge." Mary sifted through the snow as if she were able to walk on top of the powdery path. No other tracks now remained and the only sign that they were on the right path were the signs they had carved into the trees the past summer. They came to another fork in the road and Mary moved in close to the near wall of trees as she examined the next sign.

"We should be almost there. This is the crossroad." On a clear day they would have been able to see the meadow down the length of the path, but the snow was now falling heavy and the end of the path showed only white. Mary looked down on her sleeve. "Some of this snow almost looks like ash."

Ahead the silky floor of the path began to show subtle specks of grey and black. The twins looked at each other not knowing what to think. Their pace quickened as they approached the forest's edge. They should be able to see a silhouette of the house from here but saw nothing but snow. Had they taken a wrong turn and ended up in another meadow? Max went back to check the nearby trees and found the carved marks that Franz had placed months ago.

A brisk walk soon turned into a run across the meadow as they neared where the house should be. The snow darkened ahead and the smell of burnt wood and oil, which started as only a faint hint, now saturated the air. Max yelled out and then disappeared into the snow below. Mary turned and saw nothing. Staring in the direction of the yell she saw Max slowly rising from the meadow's snowy floor with a deformed gear the size of his foot in hand. The other hand was rubbing his toe, which had found the remnant of the great machine. "This is from the machine room." Max turned it over, trying to grasp how it could have been bent to its present form. "We reconnected it to the machine's center only yesterday." Even in the thick snow he could see blast marks on the warped metal. "I think there was an explosion."

The two continued forward, careful not to trip over debris that cluttered their path at every step. Closer in they could now see the smoldering remnants of the house's walls. Some fires still burned but most had now been smothered by the heavy snowfall. Only a small portion of the manger still lay intact. Betsy and the rest of the cattle now huddled there trying to stay warm and out of the weather.

The twins looked at each other and then ran into what was left of the house looking for John and Franz but saw nothing. They yelled their names as they turned over smoking wood planks, but their cries were drowned in the snow. The wind was now blowing harder. They returned to what was left of the manger.

If they were to search any farther they would need to wait for the storm to pass. They huddled down in the hay with the cows and wept. In the corner of what was left of the manger stood the wooden statue of Becky, now half burnt, her legs still smoldering. Her charred arm reached out toward the children as if to urge them to leave before it was too late. As if to answer, the wind howled and the snow began to fall heavier.

CHAPTER 18

The Song

Franz tensed as the great bear opened his jaws, their massive size spanning the full height of the boy. The teeth were like heavy white spears and as the bear neared, Franz could see deep gouges like the heavy wear of a sword that had seen too many battles. The great mouth now hovered over John's charred body as if the bear was preparing to take one fatal bite and tear him in half. Franz pulled back his knife for one great lunge at the bear, but then caught the bear's eye in his and held his blade, not knowing why.

The bear's tongue emerged from behind the teeth and probed John's body like a surgeon making ready for the first cut. The bear then began to lick the charred back. The massive tongue went back and forth over John's broken body, sweeping over Franz's feet like the tide pulling back over a rocky shore. Franz could feel the many scars on the tongue as they rolled across his feet, each promising a story of its own. His toes felt warm, but deeper, like a fire in his bones. Franz looked down at his feet and saw the charred flesh now falling off John like the shell of an egg revealing healthy pink skin beneath. The healthy flesh spread like a pool of clean water washing over a stone with the charred flesh now falling away.

It was then that the great bear's lips began to whisper a song so faint that Franz leaned in closer to hear. At first he could not make out the words but could only follow the melody that built on itself, getting louder as it went.

* * * * *

At a time known only to John his mind awakened with a fiery jolt. In his mind's eye he saw himself as an infant held tight to his mother's bosom. She was rocking him and he could hear a faint song in the back of his mind, but she was not singing. He saw her as if he were a fly in the corner of the ceiling and there in the opposite corner of the room was the great bear of his dreams curled up in a massive ball of fur watching over the mother and child.

The tone of the song shifted and John was now watching himself as a young boy playing with his father in the field. Lying in the meadow blowing fluff off the flowers was the great bear, still watching. John focused hard on the bear and could make out that the bear was singing the song he heard in his head. He watched as his younger self danced in the flowers of the field and now could see that he was dancing in beat to the music of the bear.

The tone of the music darkened as the scene changed to the funeral of his mother and the darker years that followed. The great bear walked alongside with his younger self, all the time singing. John could remember the emptiness of his heart in those years but was surprised that the bear also seemed to be sad and the mood of the song that drove the action of those in the vision reflected that sadness. As the years played on, John began to lose focus on himself and now concentrated more on the bear that seemed to be orchestrating and at the same time sharing his life.

The melody picked up as he watched himself and Becky living in the house together. John took his eye off the bear for a moment to watch Becky with a longing eye. The tone of the music soured and John again found himself at a funeral, this time Becky's. The music further darkened as he found himself alone working on the clocks and devising the machine that ran the house. The song was now so soft he needed to strain to make it out. He searched the workroom frantically for the bear, now desperately longing for that which only a day prior he had feared with all his soul, but the bear could not be seen. Then he looked out the window at the distant tree line and as the moon emerged from a cloud he saw the sheen of the great bear's coat at the forest's edge. He was left to watch himself working on a clock, dreaming of a mechanical world, and the loneliness of the sight overtook him and nearly swallowed him whole. He urged himself to go out and find the bear, but he had no voice in his vision and the man that was himself continued with his work on the gears in the house, not hearing the warning call. Just before he lost himself in the darkness of himself the music grew louder and he saw himself at the forest's edge in the fog searching for Betsy.

As if floating over the area he watched his vision self surrounded by fog. All around him circled a pack of wolves darting in and out as if to test him, and then like water circling a drain they converged on him. John cringed as he watched himself bit and torn. Then from the distance he saw the back of the great bear plowing through the fog toward the carnage. Sensing the approaching bear, the wolves left John in a bloody heap and attacked the bear like an angry swarm of bees. The great bear was not defenseless and split one of the wolves in two with his massive jaws.

A purple mist released from what had been the wolf and seeped into the earth. The other wolves were relentless, clawing and biting at the bear without regard to their growing casualties. When enough of the dismembered wolves lay strewn on the forest floor, what was left of the pack retreated down the wide path leading into the forest.

The great bear was now bloodied from head to claw, the once regal fur coat torn and matted down with his own blood. John watched as the bear moved slowly toward his own bloodied body and knelt down by John, rubbing his fur into John's open wounds. The blood of the two mingled and many of the worst tears partially healed but not all. It was then that a hooded figure in a monk's robe led Betsy to John's body and hefted him on top of Betsy. The hooded figure reached out and touched the bear on the cheek but the bear motioned him back to John. John reached out to help the bear but he was in a vision and found only air. As his bloodied body was hauled back to the farm he looked down at his current self and saw his body now covered with the blood of the bear. The blood seeped into his skin, leaving it a half shade darker and it was then that his mind clouded.

John awoke out of the trance. He was naked in a nest of pine needles with his charred skin scattered in jagged pieces all around him. The great bear stood only a foot away watching John as he had in his dreams. Before John could think what he was doing he sprang up to the bear and clung to one of his mighty legs and wept. Never had he seen anything so lovely as the bear, never loved someone so deeply. Like a child crying out for the first time a desire was born deep within John that would forever define him. It was then that the bear spoke.

"It was not the first time that I bled for you, John. I am Soman. Take the clothes hung on the tree behind you and follow me."

It was only then that John recognized that he was naked. John looked to the tree and saw a brown robe and boots like Father Aeneas's for both himself and Franz. Beneath them was the halberd that John had brought with him when he was attacked by the wolves. As John put on the monk's robe Franz approached the bear with his knife now by his side. "My name is Franz. If my father trusts you then I will trust you." Franz then gave Soman a hug.

"I have known you before I sang your song, Franz. I have looked forward to this moment for a long time." Soman swung his giant paw around Franz, playfully throwing him up on his back. "You are wise to trust in John and in me. Ride with me while I show you my forest."

"What about Max and Mary?" Franz looked back into meadow now blowing with snow. "Can we go find them?"

"We will see them again when life returns to the forest. Do not worry for them, little one, they are being taken care of. For now they must remain on the wide path until their time comes to join us." The great bear then turned from the white meadow and walked straight toward the thick wall of trees that guarded the forest.

John followed and was amazed as he watched the trees and surrounding vines spread as if there were an invisible plow spreading the forest in front of them. Soman walked into the path that was being formed only yards in front of him. The path opened wide enough for Soman to pass but no wider. The floor of the path was soft but firm dirt, not the tangle of roots that John would have expected. He paused for a moment and looked back and could see the path closing in behind them just as it had opened. The trees gracefully slid back into position without rustling a single leaf that hung overhead.

"Do not linger, John." Soman pushed ahead effortlessly. "The narrow path only goes forward and it stops for no one."

The trees closing in were catching up to John and he quickened his pace. Light from above shone down on the wall of trees to his left and right, which rose like a white wall, the trees as tight as blades of grass in the meadow. He looked up and saw that an opening in the canopy above followed them, allowing the sky to share in Soman's journey through the forest.

"What happens if you get caught in the closing trees behind?" John again looked behind at the trees flooding back in on the path behind him like a river rushing back into its dry bed after being set free from a dam.

"Those caught lingering on the path are swallowed into the darkness of the forest. The path stops for no one." There was a tinge of sadness as Soman spoke the words.

CHAPTER 19

Learning the Song

As the day drew to a close Soman's path came to a small circular clearing. The great bear went to the middle of the circle and sat up, playfully sliding Franz off his back. "How do your feet feel, Franz?" Soman smiled.

Franz looked down at his feet and wiggled his toes. Although it was the middle of the winter they felt warm, as if he had been walking on hot stones. As Franz took his first step forward he bounded a yard ahead. He dug his toes into the soft warm earth and kneeled down to touch the top of his feet where Soman's tongue had slid over them earlier that day.

Soman began to sing a soft song and a few of the snow laden trees began to bud. The bark on the small branches creaked with joy as green leaves emerged from freshly sprouting buds. John watched as tree after tree came into bloom. He felt as if he were in the middle of an orchard at the moment it blossomed. The air was filled with the fresh clean smell of new foliage. John looked far above at the golden hue of twilight rimmed by a pink and white circle of cherry blossoms at the trees' peaks. It was far higher than a cherry tree should ever grow, with blossoms touching the sky, but nothing today seemed impossible.

"Climb that tree, Franz, and bring us down some cherries." Soman looked toward a tree adorned with a spiral of bright green leaves, their edges painted gold from the evening light above. Two small sacks were at its base that Franz picked up and tucked under his belt.

Franz bounded over to the tree and looked up at the lowest hanging limb, twice his height off the ground. Without hesitation he squatted down and then leaped straight up, overshooting the limb and catching the next one up in its place. He hung from the branch for a moment and looked down at Soman with a grin as his golden bush of hair blew with the leaves in the breeze.

Soman nodded in response and looked up to the top of the tree, which was now dark red with cherries. He licked his lips as he watched Franz tentatively leap from one branch to the next, each movement becoming more graceful than the next. Once he found his bearing, he moved like a squirrel on the young tender limbs, using the bounce off the branch for the next leap. Soon a bag brim full of cherries fell to the soft grass below. Soman scooped up a handful and handed them to John. He then took a handful for himself and raised it to the sky, and sang a short song of thanks before letting three to four cherries drop into his mouth at a time. The bag was soon empty but another bag fell from the sky, this time stained with cherry juice and marked with small red fingerprints.

Soman began to laugh. "If you eat too many cherries that high you will be too heavy to make your way down."

Franz began spiraling down the circle of trees that surrounded Soman and John, slowly making his way to the ground. By the time he got down the second bag was empty. Franz picked it up, clearly disappointed, but he said nothing.

Soman laughed again and walked over to the wall of trees and pounded three trees with one blow of his paw. The circle of trees vibrated around the circle and then up to the sky. The tree tops became a blur once the shock wave hit them and then the sky turned a dark red as if a storm had suddenly formed overhead. Soon the grass below was covered with cherries and the three ate until they were content.

John looked over to Franz still picking one cherry at a time and plopping it in his mouth. He then motioned to the trees up above. "How is all of this possible? How was Franz able to go up there?"

"A child's trust and love is easily won. He believes without asking why." Soman picked a cherry pit out from between his teeth with one of his claws.

"But what of the trees moving for the path and then blooming in midwinter here? I don't understand." John looked like a man caught in a dream that he did not want to leave.

Soman smiled and picked up a branch full of dark green leaves that had dropped in the torrential rain of cherries. A warm breeze blew through it and the leaves danced about on the branch in joy from the warm relief.

"Open your eyes to the leaves and open your ears to the song and you will understand."

John stared at the leaves as they seemed to move at random in the breeze, but as he followed them he saw that they were really moving to the rhythm of a song so faint that it only tickled his ears. As John focused on the song it began to grow louder. It was a song, similar to the song that Soman had sung of his life this morning, but far richer. As he let the song saturate his mind he saw glimpses of flowered meadows and mountain peaks and the great expanse of the ocean. Each vision only lasted a moment, keeping with the melody of the song, but the song was so vast he had no hope of catching all of the notes. He then focused back at the leaves and the world slowed down.

It was only then that he saw that the leaves were not really moving at all. The song and the air seemed to mix at the edge of a moment, creating new leaves and replacing the ones before them moment by moment. The leaves were not a thing being moved by the song, it was the song itself mixing with the air. Soon John could see this movement on an entire branch.

What he had seen before as a branch moving randomly in the wind he now saw as many different branches, one created moment by moment after the other by the song mixing with the fabric of the air itself. He then looked up at the treetops and saw that the whole forest was moving with the song … *was* the song. A beautiful work of art created moment by moment. As he reached up toward the sky wanting to be part of the music he saw his arm was also part of the song. He quickly pulled his arm back to feel his skin, but he felt the same as he always had. As he looked to Soman for the answer to his unasked question he realized that the source of the song was the great bear himself.

John looked back at his hand, moving his fingers in sequence as he used to when his view of the world was more simplistic and mechanical. "What would happen if the song stopped?"

Soman was now rolling in the grass playing a game with Franz, who giggled in the background. "Look up to the sky, John." Soman closed his eyes and the melody of the greater song grew darker.

John saw past the dark blue of the sky deep into the dark space beyond. His vision passed the sun, where he saw the song dancing in the fire at the edge of the yellow orb as the song mixed with the fabric of empty space, replacing the brilliance of the fiery ball from one moment to the next. Deeper and deeper into the emptiness of space he went until he came to another star ten times the size of the sun. It seemed to dance as it moved with the song, mixing with the canvas of space moment by moment, a great piece of art in itself, with towers of flame stretching out to the dark boarders of space as if reaching out to the great bear far, far away.

John watched as the song faded. A dark sadness gripped him as the star dissolved to nothing when the song that had sustained it left. There was no explosion or dusty mess left afterward, only the sad darkness of space left behind. John did not know why he should feel sadness for the loss of the star that he had not even known to exist earlier that day, but he was grieved and tears welled in his eyes.

Soman grabbed him with his arm and pulled him in to his warm furry side as the vision faded and John returned to the forest. "I will teach you how to sing ... not the great song that sustains the world, for you are a part of that song, but instead a song in harmony with that song."

Into the night Soman did what he had said he would do—he taught John how to sing. At first it was difficult. Soman would tell him to clear his mind, a task easier said than done. "The mind is always filled with something, as is the heart. You can only hope to choose what to fill the mind with. The heart is another matter."

John thought of the most beautiful thing he could, something of his choosing to fill his mind. A week ago it would have been gears or springs or the memory of Becky or even the children that had become his own. As his mind searched for beauty it was overwhelmed by a single image, that of Soman. As he began to sing again he did not think about the words that would come, he only contemplated the beauty of Soman. Soon the song became a stream of consciousness that John shared with the song itself as if the song existed separate from John and yet was woven into the deepest part of himself. The song spoke of the majesty of Soman and his great love that had allowed him to suffer for John's sake. The song was beautiful and when he was finished both he and Soman were in tears, so moving was the song.

"This is now part of your song, John. In the morning you will be ready to begin the narrow path. Tonight we will sleep under the stars."

John lay awake for an hour staring at the stars above. He remembered a similar night in the heat of the summer as he had contemplated the mechanical underpinnings of the stars' wonderful movements. How he could have been so blind at the time was beyond him now. He now saw the stars moving across the sky, living only moment by moment, sustained by the great song. His mind then drifted to the star that had died that night, and as his eyes shut his soul pirouetted down a narrow line between sorrow and joy wondering how deep the rabbit hole would take him.

CHAPTER 20

Dead Ends

The storm raged on through the night and Max and Mary were forced to stay in what was left of the house with the cattle overnight. Dawn came with a pink glow in the east and it was in that light that the twins again searched the charred remains for their family but found nothing. They returned to the house and salvaged what provisions remained and put them in a sack to carry with them. It would be death to stay at the charred remains of the house and the village had nothing to offer them with Father Aeneas now gone. They looked out to the forest, the only home they had left, and began making their way toward it. To their left Mary saw an indentation in a nearby snow bank and they walked closer to examine it. The meadow and the land near the farm were covered with a foot of powdery snow, but even that amount of snowfall could not hide the deep trudging path that John had taken the morning before to the forest.

Max examined the tracks. They were only a day old. "John must have made it out of the house. There is blood mixed with the ice on the bottom of the tracks. He was hurt. The tracks are heavy, even for John. He must have been carrying something."

Mary looked at Max, hope in her eyes. The tracks were not hard to follow since the sky was clear. They led to the forest's edge, where they found a nest of charred skin and the tracks of John and Franz. Mary hugged Max, both of them sobbing. The two had made it out alive. John's tracks led to a tree, turned around and then went straight into a wall of trees. Franz's tracks ended near the nest. No other footprints were to be found.

"They could not have just walked into that." Mary grabbed the tree where John's last footprint ended and shook it. They must have doubled back on the wide path. Its entrance is just over there." Mary pointed down a row of trees.

"They didn't go back in the meadow." Max looked back over the smooth field of white. "We would have seen John's tracks. There is only one way to go." Max lifted up their sack and the two began another adventure on the forest paths, this time hunting for something much more precious than game.

CHAPTER 21

Kytann the Great Wolf

Deep within the forest was a dark place where the souls of men dared not tread. Its boundaries were vast and marked by the stench of decay and death. If one could peer through the darkness, miles of a desolate plain would be seen. Huge ancient trees older than the age of man lifted up into the darkness and provided the blanket above that kept out the sun. This open land was studded with rotted stumps of trees, ripped down at their base many years ago by the jaws of a terrible beast. The stars of the night had long forsaken this place, the only light to be seen in the glassy eyes of the wolves prowling this land in the service of their master. In the middle of this dark land, a land that had not seen the joy of the sun since the creation of the world, lay a cave, the dwelling place of a great wolf, Kytann.

Kytann was a monstrous wolf, ten times the size of the hundreds of grey wolves that served him in the darkness of the forest. His coat was coal black, revealing his stature as one of the original fallen, with only a small tuft of white on his left forepaw to distinguish him from the great wolf who lingered not in the forests but in the cities of men. Kytann shivered at the thought of the dark one, both terrible and cunning. He owed his freedom from the bear to the dark one, his allegiance pledged in eons of bloodshed, but it was better to keep a distance from that terrible force if possible.

Kytann stretched his neck left and right in the great cave that was his home, trying to release a nerve that pinched near the top of his spine. It had been nearly three hundred years since the battle that had nearly lost him his head. The sword fell hard and if it had been but a foot higher death from this world would have found him. But as fate would have it, the sword hit a vertebra at the base of his neck, fracturing it. Kytann healed fast, but not all things healed in this world and he was left with a pain that ran from the cursed bone to his left forepaw, as if to remind him on a daily basis of the small impurity that remained within him. This lingering injury gave him a twitch and his head would jerk slightly to the left and to the right when he was agitated. It made the lowly half bred wolves who served him nervous. He took pleasure in that.

It was that same nervousness that led him into the forest, away from the dark one, to wait out this war that waged without end. Men were good sport, but even that now bored him. For three hundred years he had made this forest his own, a haven of dark solitude. But the bear who was not a bear had ruined that for him. It was the bear that the dark one had freed him from, from an eternity of slavery. Kytann once had had dreams of what freedom would bring him, but he had settled for dark solitude and now even that was threatened by the bear. Kytann's great head twitched back and forth at the thought. Was taking the form of a bear meant to mock his choice to take the form of a wolf? His head shook again, his red eyes raging. The dark one was waiting for something but Kytann was tired of waiting. The light grew closer and closer to his haven as the years grew on. It was a mistake for the bear who was not a bear to linger in his forest. The bear must die.

The only question was how. His recent trap for the bear using the farmer for bait had failed. Where had the bear taken John? He had invested years filling that man's head with mechanical visions of the truth, a truth that he had paid dearly for. And what did that farmer do with the ultimate truth of the universe? He built that monstrosity of a house. At least it kept him busy and out of the deep of the forest, which of course had been his intent in the first place.

A scuffling sound could be heard at the entrance of the cave. Kytann's body tensed as he listened. It was two of the lesser wolves. His muscles rippled as he sprang like a bolt of lightning to the front of the cave. He could unleash a great growl and startle the "grey coats" as he called them, but instead he stood tall and released his breath, alerting them to his presence with the warm exhale. The two wolves, startled, turned and lowered their heads.

"Master, the two older children that walked the wide paths with the brown coat are now in the forest alone. We saw them make camp."

Kytann paused for a moment. "And what of John, the man in the farm, and the younger child?"

"We did not see them, but we found where they disappeared into the thick of the forest."

Kytann nodded, deep in thought. "So the bear took the youngest and the oldest and left the twins to die in the cold of the forest."

"Shall we kill them, Master?

"Was it not I that freed you from the slavery of this world? Do not presume to know my mind." Kytann leaned into the pair of wolves who cowered lower on the ground. It was better for them to be reminded of their place. "Lead them deeper into the forest, lead them to me."

"But what of the ghost that runs through the trees?" The two wolves lowered their heads awaiting the wrath of their master, but the ghost had killed many of their kind and he would surely be close.

"Let him be drawn in also and we will clean the forest of this encroaching light once and for all."

CHAPTER 22

The Narrow Path

Before the morning light broke John awoke from the first peaceful sleep he had had in many years. Soman and Franz were still sleeping. Unable to stay still, he began to walk the perimeter of trees that circled the three. Running his hands over the trees, he thought, they feel no different than they have in the past, but they *are* different. They were different because now he knew their true nature and how they were sustained moment by moment by the song of the bear.

As he studied the trees a calmness set in, and he began to focus on Soman. He began to sing of Soman as he was taught the night before. This morning it was of the image of Soman's compassion for the star that was lost last night. He felt the warmth of his embrace during that dark moment and without thinking he took a step forward as the narrow path opened in the wall of trees.

As the trees closed behind him Soman smiled with one eye half open, watching. Franz pulled closer to the great bear's warmth and Soman tucked him in tight with his arm. He closed his eyes without worry. There was still an hour before daylight and it was time to sleep. He was now in the hands of the Old One. The path would lead him to where he needed to go.

John walked through the forest without a care in the world. The peace of the night was still with him as he sang on. As light began to break he turned around to head toward camp. Doubling back ten paces, he came to the tail of the path that had followed him on his walk.

He focused on Soman and reached out to the way he had come but the trees continued to close in on him. As the trees converged his hand became caught between the trailing wedge of forest. He pulled on his arm as he looked behind him toward what was the front of the path. It, too, was now closing in from the front. Fear set in as the air grew heavy in his contracting tomb of wood. The path now narrowed, pressing in on his body and squeezing out what was left of his breath. With all his might he pulled his arm free and turned to the front of the path, singing the song. As he did the path halted, widened and began to move forward again as if nothing had happened.

It was then that John remembered Soman telling him the path waited for no one. Realizing he was not in control of the path, John walked on several steps. The path opened back to their camp as Soman and Franz were beginning to wake. It had not occurred to him that he might get lost in the thick of the forest, but without trying he had circled back to Soman. The path had found its own way back, raising a question in John's mind as to whether he led the path or it led him.

Soman and Franz awoke quickly with no lingering tiredness of sleep. Soman motioned John back to the trees. John hesitated as he met Soman's eyes, contemplating whether he wanted to go back on the narrow path, but Soman would not have hesitation and nudged him back to the wall of trees where John quieted his mind and began to sing a song of Soman that almost seemed to feed itself. His mind filled with the beauty of Soman and once again the trees gave way to the narrow path.

The two walked for about an hour with Franz still riding on Soman's back until they came to a small clearing near the edge of a narrow rushing river. The water was clear and fresh, spanning twenty yards to the other side. The fast moving current rushed over smooth rocks that stubbornly held their ground as they had for thousands of years.

Soman jumped into the cold water with the eagerness of a child who was about to enter a new game. Water splashed over Franz, drenching his great mop of hair. He clung tight to Soman, smiling as Soman swung his forepaw though the water as if he were dancing. His paw caught a fish and swung it to the clearing by John. Franz waved his free arm about with joy, joining in the dance, and motioned for John to join them. Franz's wet hair whipped left and right as Soman's great paws swung deep into the water, bringing up a fish with every swing. One out of three made it to the shore. The others were tossed high in the air where Soman caught them in his mouth and swallowed them whole.

John listened carefully and could hear a song of thanks for the fish in rhythm with the rush of the water. The energy of the dance was contagious and he waded into the water to join the dance. Once John was waist high in the rushing water he felt his feet giving way to the sandy bottom as he began to slide downstream. His foot found a smooth rock and he nearly lost his footing.

A familiar panic began to seep into his heart as the image of being crushed by the tree flashed through his mind. He reached his arm toward the great bear, who had not stopped his dance but instead, seemed to have picked up the beat, stomping on a large rock in the middle of the river. Water shot straight up like a geyser with each beat.

As the water splashed on John from the pounding of the rock his panic gave way to the rhythm of the paw on the old rock. Without thinking about what was happening, he felt his mind clear. He felt the age of the rock and the sway of the river as his toes dug into the bed of sand. Without realizing what he was doing he began to sing the song of the narrow path, and just as the trees made way in the forest so did the water of the river. He made his way up to Soman and began to throw his arms into the water as Soman did and they both threw fish to the shore.

When the dance was done the three moved back to the shore and John lit a fire to cook some of the fish for Franz and himself. With his knives Franz filleted many fish and set them out to dry. As they sat to eat John sang a song of thanks and there were no fish left after the breakfast feast. Once John and Franz had dried out Soman pointed them toward the forest's edge. To the rhythm of John's song the two disappeared into the trees for the first of many day-long runs through the forest.

CHAPTER 23

Two Weeks Later

Father Aeneas awoke in a small grassy clearing as twilight painted the world gold. He grabbed a small sack and placed some dried meat and cheese in it. The twins' rations that they had brought from John's barn had run out yesterday. He did not know how long they were to wander the wide paths but his instructions were clear: "Look after them without them seeing you, keep them safe from the wolves." The wolves' activity had picked up pace and if the last week was any indicator as to how tonight would go it was going to be a busy night. He looked back at his rations. He had three days' tops if he shared with the twins. There was no worry in his mind as he picked up his sword and opened the narrow path.

Father Aeneas picked up his pace to a trot, holding his broad sword at the ready over his shoulder. He looked up for a moment at the stars through the small opening above that chased him through the forest. How long had he been holding back the wolves in the forest? He had lost track of the years. He remembered the first day he had met Soman while on a journey through the woods. He had nearly soiled himself as he had turned and run. It had taken only seconds for Soman to bowl him over and pin him to the ground. Opening his mouth he had let out a great roar, which in retrospect was playful. The priest chuckled. It had not seemed so playful at the time.

He remembered the first words that Soman had spoken to him. "Brother, why do you run? I have work for you to do." And that had been the beginning … the narrow path suddenly opened into the side of a wide path that crossed it.

Aeneas kept his pace. Four wolves turned in surprise as he ran toward them, their eyes glowing in the night. The eyes made it easier to find the neck, he thought. The sword swung to the left leaving two wolves headless. Without breaking stride the sword swung around to the right and with the next blow two more heads laid on the ground. Coming to the wall of trees on the other side of the wide path he leapt into the trees. The narrow path opened and the forest swallowed him without hesitation as if it were happy to play its part in ridding itself of the wolves that infested its borders.

Where was he? Oh yes, the beginning. It had been odd at first trusting in the narrow path, trees constantly closing in, but it now felt warm and secure. The path had always led him to where he needed to go, even if it was not where he thought he should be going at the time. He remembered arriving at the village and by default running the parish all those years, priest by day, hunter by night. He would have preferred to have just stayed in the forest with Soman, but then he would have never met John and the children. It was during those years that he learned the narrow path did not end at the forest's edge. Once on the path, always on the path. It was just easier to see in the dense forest.

The narrow path suddenly opened again into the wide path, this time next to the children's camp. He smiled as he tossed the provisions he had packed toward Mary but did not slow his pace, leaping once more into the forest and back on the narrow path.

The children … they were a blessing. He had forgotten before he had taken them on what it was like to have a family. It was good that Soman had a plan for them. He wondered how long he would be called to cleanse the forest. The work had been hard and not every night went without bite or claw tearing his flesh. The path had never given him more than what he could handle, but that did not guarantee that he would not shed blood. And shed he did, especially in the early years. His hand rubbed the length of his arm feeling more scar than smooth skin. One day the path would open and he would not reenter. The peace of death would find …

The path opened again, interrupting his thoughts, this time leading him lengthwise down the wide path. These were not his favorite runs. Coming around a corner, three wolves appeared in the night. *Thank you, Soman, for the bright eyes.* The sword fell left and right. He kept up the pace, leaving the dead wolves headless behind. Turning another corner six wolves lay waiting. They were getting smarter. Was this their idea of a trap? He raised his sword and the wolves converged on him. One caught his free arm in his jaws. The sword fell on two wolves in front. The wolf on his left arm pulled him to the side. He turned and the sword raised and fell, killing two more at his rear. He then raised his sword and pulled the wolf that that had his arm tight in its jaws close so he could look the wolf in the eyes. The sword fell and then the wolf's body fell, leaving the head clenched on his arm. He raised his arm with the head still attached like a trophy. The last wolf fled and the priest disappeared back onto the narrow path.

Death. Yes, it comes to us all, he thought, as he pried the wolf's head from his arm and tied a bandage over it. But the peace of death would not find him today. His left arm throbbed as he kept pace on the path. The path would not end at death this day. This he knew. As he ran under the stars that night he mused over what the path would be like on the other side of that doorway. His arm throbbed, but he hardly noticed, his mind immersed in the path beyond.

CHAPTER 24

Later That Night

Kytann lay quietly outside of his cave waiting for news of the children. The pack that he had sent to drive them into the dark domain that was his home should be back by now. He tilted his head over the cliff to his right to listen to the rush of water in the river far below. The sound of the water soothed him, reminding him of a song that he had written before the escape from the light. It was a happier time and a happier place. He had written many songs in those days for the Old One, telling of his glorious deeds. He began to hum a song that he had thought was long forgotten to the rhythm of the river below. He was happy then. Why was it that he had left? The promise of freedom, freedom to follow his own will.

In the middle of that thought a single wolf sprayed with the deep purple of demon wolf blood climbed near. Kytann frowned. "I see that you met with the brown ghost."

The wolf who had no name lowered his head, hiding his eyes from Kytann's glare.

"How many did he kill tonight?" Kytann slowly rose to his feet, looming over the minion wolf. He had not bothered to name any but one. One was the same as the other, expendable in the service of the greater good, his good.

The wolf continued to look away.

"All were lost save you?" Kytann was now directly over the lesser wolf, who cowered in the dirt. His head ratcheted to the left and right. "And the children. The twins. Are they any closer to the dark regions of the forest?"

"We were not able to get close enough to drive them, my lord." The wolf kept his head low avoiding any eye contact. Bad news was rarely taken well. The twitching made it worse. The wolf pictured himself being bit in half and thrown into the river below. It would not have been the first time that such tidings were received in such a way. "The cursed brown one comes from nowhere and then disappears into the dense of the forest. His metal kills all that it touches. They say he cannot die."

Kytann let out a howl that shook the dark field of the forest. "He is just a man. A monk in the service of the bear. He is not immortal." Kytann thought of crushing this cowardly thing on the rocks below. "I should have killed that monk when I sent the sickness through the village. He and his master have mocked me for long enough." Kytann was now speaking with a voice that filled the darkness. "Bring me Sir William." He would have his revenge soon. But first he needed leverage. Leverage to bring the bear and that brown menace into the darkness of the forest. A smile crept on his long face, his eyes glowing red. Both children would be nice, but one would be enough. Perhaps it would be easier and more effective to split them up.

Sir William came into view from the path that led to his cave. He had been the alpha of the pack before Kytann had changed the wolves to better serve his needs. At first it was a private joke to give one of these lowly creatures a name, but it grew on him over time. "Sir William, it is time for us to take back the forest. Listen carefully to what you must do. And under no circumstances are the children to be hurt—yet."

CHAPTER 25

The Monk

Mary awoke next to a smoldering fire. Max was still sleeping next to her. Her stomach growled reminding her of her last meal a day prior. She reached over for her bow and there next to it she saw a cloth bag.

"Max, get up." Mary snapped to her feet and nudged the sack, not knowing what to think.

Max rolled over grabbing his bow, and drew an arrow as he looked left and right. "What did you see? Where is it?"

Mary pointed to the sack as she approached it. "It was there when I awoke." Mary peaked in through the top. "It looks like cheese."

The two picked up the sack and without thinking began to eat. With a mouth full of cheese Max looked to Mary. "Where do you think it came from?"

Mary shook her head as she headed down the path to investigate. There were more dead wolves only twenty yards down, their heads severed like those they had found over the past several weeks. She picked up one of the heads by its ear and showed it to Max. "A clean cut at the base of the neck. The footprints start from that edge of the path and disappear on that side." Mary pointed to the wall of trees that bordered the wide path shaking her head.

Ahead, the path came to a crossroad. Max caught up with Mary as she looked down at the wolf tracks. Some were fresh from last night and went in two directions. "We split up and go a hundred yards each way then meet back here."

Mary nodded. She drew an arrow in her bow. Hunting had been poor the farther into the forest they went. Fresh tracks meant a next meal, even if it was wolf.

Once the twins had disappeared down the two paths a dozen wolves emerged from the third pathway. They tentatively stood at the crossroads as they had been told, looking down all the paths with watchful eyes. It was rare that they would be this far on the paths during the light of day but the master had said it was necessary risk to rid themselves of the brown menace. They had passed their brothers' heads on the path up. Fear and anger saturated the air. The wolves sniffed the children's tracks. They had promised Kytann that the children would be delivered unharmed. But what Kytann did not know would not hurt him … or them.

Max turned a corner, his bow drawn. He missed hunting alongside Mary but they had agreed that they could cover more area this way. Up ahead he saw the hind end of a lame wolf dragging his right leg. Max quickened his pace. As he turned the corner he saw the wolf limping down the path. He took aim but before he loosed his arrow Sir William looked back at him with tired eyes and spoke.

"Did you enjoy your breakfast? I lost many brothers delivering it to you." Sir William embellished the lie with enough bitterness to make it ring true.

Max kept the arrow drawn with the wolf still in his sights. "How is it that you can talk, and why would you help us?"

"Our master Kytann cares for all living things. You search for your younger brother and the farmer. They have been taken by our enemy, the great bear of the forest. Kytann seeks your help in freeing them and killing the bear. The same bear that nearly killed the farmer."

Max nodded his head as he slowly lowered the arrow. "If what you say is true then we will help you. We must go back to get my sister."

Sir William nodded. He would have both the twins after all. Kytann would be pleased.

* * * * *

Mary had gone as far down the path as she had always done. The wolf tracks continued off into the distance. If she were to go further she would need to get Max. The trails were tricky and it would be easy for them to get lost.

From her rear she heard the brush of fur on a bush. She drew her arrow, sighted the wolf, and shot. The arrow struck true, finding the wolf's heart. Purple seeped into the snow as eleven other wolves turned the bend. Seeing their brother freshly killed in the snow, they quickened their pace. Their revenge had waited long enough. Kytann would have his prize and they would have theirs.

Mary backed away slowly and drew another arrow. She doubted that she would have time to draw another. As the wolves spread out to cover the width of the path she picked what looked like the leader and ran the arrow between his eyes.

The pack howled and converged toward Mary. Before the first wolf reached her she heard a rustling in the trees as a monk with a broad sword sprang out from a path that came from nowhere in the forest. The wolves froze in their tracks at the sight of their menace. He opened one arm and grabbed Mary at the waist and with the other let the sword fall, killing the two nearest wolves to Mary. He carried Mary to the opposite wall of the trail and leapt toward the dense wall of trees.

Mary closed her eyes awaiting impact but felt none. When she opened her eyes she found she was being carried down a narrow path by a monk that looked suspiciously similar to Father Aeneas.

"I see that you are hunting alone, Mary." Father Aeneas set her down gently on the soft soil of the path. He brushed back her hair and smiled. "I thought we agreed that you and Max would always hunt as a pair."

Mary wrapped her arms around the monk and hugged him.

Father Aeneas looked back at the tail of the path closing behind them. "We must get moving, Mary. This path waits for no one."

Mary looked back and saw the path disappearing behind her, and began running after Father Aeneas. "But what about Max?" Mary reached out and touched the monk on the shoulder but he did not slow his pace. "We must go back and get him."

"There is no going back on the narrow path, Mary." The Father quickened his pace. "Max is now in the hands of the Old One. You have much to learn, and we have little time. For now all you need know is that you must quicken your pace."

With a heavy heart Mary ran to catch up. The soil beneath her feet felt warm as she ran and the path had a clean breeze that she had not smelled for weeks. She looked up at the trees separating above letting in the welcome warmth of the sun, and the heaviness of her heart lightened as she fell into the rhythm of the run. The priest had never let her down in the past, and she would have to trust him as she had in the past.

CHAPTER 26

Fellowship on The Path

John awoke on the soft grass near the edge of the river. The middle of the river still rumbled and sprayed where he and Soman had fished several weeks back, but the water near the side of the stream was still this morning. The first light of dawn reflected down on the water and it sparked in all colors of the rainbow. John reached down and scooped up a handful of water and drank, and a calm washed over him. The days now ran together as he and Franz ran the narrow path, but the narrow path was anything but routine. One never knew what you might find as the path opened up. Every moment on the path was an adventure.

John walked over to Franz and woke him. Together they ate dried fish and berries that grew in the green oasis that Soman had provided them. Soman had now been gone for three days, disappearing into the woods. He would never say where he went. Although John and Franz were content with each other's company they were always happy to see him back.

After eating the two headed toward the trees and found John's old halberd remade with a long dark shaft leaning against a young sapling. The metal of the ax was now heavier and as John ran his finger over the blade it seemed dull. An inscription was engraved on the side of the ax, but neither John nor Franz could read the strange language it appeared to have been written in and so its meaning would have to remain a mystery until Soman returned. Near where the halberd set were Franz's throwing knives, which had also been remade with the same dark wood in the handles. They were light and their bright silver finish sparkled in the light.

John looked down at Franz, weighing the halberd in his hands. "It looks like Soman has something special for us on the path today. We had better be ready."

Franz nodded as he tucked the knives in small sheaths on his belt.

John calmed his mind and filled it with an image of Soman. What had started as just a physical image had grown into something far richer as they had shared time with him. The image now flowed with the remembrances of laughing around the fire as they went over the day's adventures on the path or listened to Soman's strange tales from long ago. He could still feel the heat given off the great bear's body as they had slept close to him on the colder nights. The image was now only a trigger for an experience that was far deeper than a picture in his mind. John's song, as it turned out, was also a trigger to the same experience. He no longer needed the song to open the path, but the song had grown on him and he hummed it as the narrow path opened.

The enriched image of Soman had its advantages on the narrow path. Without having to concentrate on the song, John was now able to run the path. When he had first begun running the path, John had been careful not to go too fast as the path would sometimes turn abruptly, and it was not infrequently that John would find himself going face first into the trees. Now he flowed with the path, no longer trying to control it, no longer distracted by the world outside the path. The two now raced through the forest, never knowing where the path would take them, whether at the end of it they might find a stone cliff to climb or an open field to cross.

"Falling behind, Franz." John smiled as he hurdled a fallen log.

Franz stayed close to John, but he was now able to open small paths from the main path as he bounced from one tree into a tunnel of wood that would appear in front of him and then pop out twenty yards ahead without warning.

Franz emerged with a wild scream as he jetted out of the path wall only a couple of feet in front of John. John laughed as he dodged out of the way. When Franz first started the game of weaving in and out of the path he would catch John unaware, mostly from behind, bowling them both down the path in the soft earth. Now John could almost sense him coming and would slow down just enough to let Franz fly out in front of him. John had now built up a good sweat which glistened off his forehead and dripped off his eyelid, and as he reached up to wipe it away he caught the gleam of metal in the path wall. He slowed his pace slightly to look back for the metal, when Franz wailed as he emerged from a hole in the wood behind him, sending them both rolling down the path. They laughed together as they stood up.

Franz was the first to notice a bronze shield crushed between two trees on their left. He reached over to touch the metal, which was now worn with what looked like more than a thousand years of weather. As he ran his finger down the curve of the shield he came to a rough spot he first mistook for small branches that had crawled over the side of the shield. As he picked one away it came off, too loose for a branch. He brought it closer to find it was a small bone from the end of a finger. Franz threw it to the ground and retreated toward John.

John looked back at the tail end of the path, which was now advancing on the two. He grabbed Franz and again began to jog keeping pace with the path, but no more. Bronze breast plates now littered the walls of the path, contorted by the branches that ran through them. As John's eye lingered on one he saw that the skeleton of a man was intertwined with the knurled wood that held captive the former owner of the armor. John knew from pictures that he had seen in the church that these were Roman soldiers from ancient times. They quickened their pace as they passed through hundreds of soldiers whose remains adorned the path with a collage of bone and bronze. Although it took only minutes to run through the area to clean wood again, they ran for what seemed like hours.

The two were breathing heavily when the path opened up to one of the wide trails of the forest. There to their left and right were nine wolves with three dead on the ground surrounded by purple snow. Two of the dead were pierced by arrows, while the third was without a head.

The nine wolves backed up for a moment, clearly startled by the intrusion.

John raised the halberd and swung in a circle, warding off several wolves slowly encroaching. Franz held his ground, looking wilder than the wolves. Without warning he pulled out three knives and threw them in sequence at the nearest wolves, sinking the blades deep in their flesh. He then pushed John toward the opposite wall of the trail and the narrow path once again opened up. The two ran in with two wolves close behind. Franz took to the air, bouncing from limb to limb, as John slowly lost ground to the wolves closing in behind. Knowing that he could not keep an even pace with the wolves, John stopped and turned, pointing the spear head of the halberd at the oncoming wolves.

The wolves slid to a stop one in front of the other, growling at John and now slowly approaching. John could see the rear of the trail now closing in and smiled. The smile took the wolves off guard and as they looked back the tail of the rear wolf was taken in by the advancing trees. Bones crushed and violet blood stained the floor of the forest as the narrow path swallowed the intruder. The other wolf watched in horror as his brother was absorbed into the forest.

This time John did not hesitate and he raised the halberd and brought the ax head down on the turned head of the remaining wolf, which fell to the ground with a soft thud. The inscription on the head of the halberd, now filled with purple blood, shone bright as if to call out to the forest that justice had been served that day. The path continued to advance and as John turned to run to keep up with the path he saw the wolf's bones crushed into the forest just as the Roman soldiers had been crushed many years ago.

John looked up at Franz, who had watched everything from above. Franz shook his fist in triumph in celebration of the foul beasts that now lay dead, enmeshed in the forest behind.

John shook his halberd in the air back at Franz in return, but did not completely share his joy. He had formerly envisioned the narrow path as a safe haven from the world outside. He was clearly mistaken, and now wondered what other evil lay ahead.

CHAPTER 27

Plans within Plans

Max returned with Sir William to the crossroad but Mary was not there. Both boy and wolf, nervous as to what they might find, headed up the path that Mary had taken. One hundred yards in they found the carnage of the wolves with only four still alive farther up the path, though they could find no arrows. The wolves had hidden them according to one of the four, who told Sir William what had occurred in the language of the wolf that Max could not understand. Sir William stood expressionless as he heard the story and then was silent for a moment before he spoke in the language Max knew.

"The brown ghost who is in league with the bear slaughtered my brothers and took your sister captive." The wolf looked down at the body of a decapitated wolf, not having to feign anger over the shedding of the pack's blood. "I fear your sister will not make it through the time of the new moon which is only four risings away." Sir William thought back to what Kytann had instructed him to say. "The bear and the ghost sacrifice an innocent to their hideous god on the night of the new moon. They will surely kill your sister then." Hiding a smile, Sir William hung his head. "I am sorry for your loss."

* * * * *

Max's heart sank at the thought of losing his sister. "We must do something to stop them." He nudged the dead body of one of the wolves, its hair matted down with blood that had already started to freeze to the ground, with his foot. "We must find my sister now!"

"I do not have the power to chase the ghost through the thick of the wood and the bear is as mighty as he is evil. We must seek the help of my master, Kytann."

"Where do we go to find this Kytann?"

Sir William began trotting back the way they came to the crossroad and took the trail leading to the deep forest. "We must go to where the ghost cannot follow, in the dark of the forest where his thick trees have been uprooted."

Max traveled with the wolves for several hours down the trail, which widened slowly as they went. He saw the trunks of trees that had been torn from their roots near the edges of the trail and the massive teeth marks on them penetrating bark and rotting wood. The way became darker as they went and the clean smell of snow was slowly replaced with the stench of urine and rotting game half eaten near the edge of the trail. It filled Max with the urge to gag. He picked up the pace. Mary could be hurting right now. *I have no time to lose.*

They came upon the dark field in mid afternoon. Hundreds of eyes followed Max as he followed the wolves up a steep hill to the mouth of a cave near a cliff. Max looked over the edge and could make out the sound of running water but he could see only a dark mist that filled the crevice below.

Deep from within the cave a voice could be heard whispering to Max. "What sorrows do you bring to share with the great Kytann, ruler of the black forest?"

Max saw a dark sheen moving at the mouth of the cave and as Kytann turned to look at him he saw for the first time the deep red eyes of the ancient spirit. "My sister is held captive by the spirit of the wood. She is everything to me. I would do anything to save her. Can you help me?"

Kytann crouched down so that he was at eye level with Max, having to hover his head just over the ground to get so low. "I, too, have lost many of my family to the cruelty of the bear and those who follow him. He is dangerous, more so than you could imagine. A single word from his mouth brings death. We have tried to rid the forest of this evil and have lost many good wolves in the process."

As desperation set in, Max pled with the great wolf. "But there must be a way. You can't just give up."

The red in Kytann's eyes flared for a moment. "I have not given up, child." Kytann rose to his full height, more than twice as tall as Max. "It is said that a black arrow fashioned from an ancient tree deep in the forest could bring the bear down." Kytann moved closer to the cliff, listening to the rushing water far below. "But even if we were to fashion such an arrow, it would have to be fired far away from the bear lest he see you and with a word kill you. It would take a great archer to do such a thing and you, Max, are still only a child."

Max took his bow from his back and one arrow from his quiver. He then reached down to the ground and found the skull of a fox in a pile of bones at the mouth of the cave. Without hesitation he threw the skull into the air and then drew an arrow and released it at the skull. One of the wolves took off down the hill as if hot on the trail of the former fox. When he returned he carried the skull pierced with an arrow between the eyes. The lesser wolf dropped the skull at the feet of Kytann, who bent down to examine what the wolf had brought.

"Perhaps we do have an archer worthy of bringing down the great and terrible bear. But we do not have much time. Only four nights remain before your sister will surely be sacrificed to the bear. We will first need to find the ancient tree from which the arrow could be formed. It is nearly two days' travel into the deep forest. I will go with you. It is a dangerous place to tread. There are larger things in this forest than myself. We shall hope they slumber as we trespass their keep."

* * * * *

Kytann gave a look to Sir William, who smiled in return. He would have to get all the details of the day's events later. He had almost given up hope of destroying the bear, but now he could nearly taste victory. He would finally have his freedom, freedom to live outside the menacing intrusions of the bear. Free to build a world of his own choosing. But first he would need to remember where he had planted the ancient tree. And they would, indeed, need to be careful. There were things that crept in the night in this cursed earth that even he feared. They would have to be careful, indeed.

77

CHAPTER 28

Running with Father Aeneas

Father Aeneas and Mary ran for over an hour before the path led them to an opening in the forest. Mary leaned over holding her knees. "What was that thing?" pointing to where they emerged from the forest.

Father Aeneas laughed as he leaned on his sword that he had planted in the ground. "That is the narrow path as it makes its way through the forest."

"We need to go back and help Max, he is alone back there." Mary pointed emphatically back from whence they came, but in truth she no longer knew in what direction to go.

Soman stepped out from the narrow path behind Mary. "Max is not alone. He is with the servant of Kytann."

Mary turned to the voice to find the great bear standing tall behind her. She jumped back, pulling an arrow from her quiver. As she pulled the arrow back ready to fire Father Aeneas ran to the bear and embraced him, burying his half bald head in Soman's fur.

Mary kept the arrow drawn aimed at the bear's left eye.

"I have seen death, little one. It holds no power over me," the great bear roared, shaking the trees surrounding them.

Mary held her ground, still not sure what to make of the talking bear. He was dangerous, to be sure, but could he help? The priest seemed to trust him, but she still held her arrow at the ready. She would need to understand the great bear before she would trust him.

"How is it that you can talk?" Mary backed up slightly, finding a more defendable position.

"I have sung before the wind whispered your name, Mary."

Not sensing the clarity that she was seeking, she asked again. "Who are you?"

Soman now spoke softly. "I am, Mary. And that is all you need to understand." Soman now slowly walked to the edge of the clearing. "Your time is limited if you want to save Max. Follow Aeneas and he will show you what you need to know."

The forest opened and Soman disappeared into the trees, leaving Aeneas and Mary alone in the clearing.

"What was that?" Mary lowered her bow.

"That was who I serve, Mary. Soman rules all that we see. I was lost in these woods before he found me and showed me the narrow path. Now I run the path in the service of the great bear, as you will, too."

Deep in thought, Aeneas picked up his sword running his hand along the side of an inscription on the blade. "Time is short, Mary."

With a sigh she picked up her old bow and quiver. Other than the clothes on her back, it was all that she had ever owned.

"When do I learn how to separate the trees?" Mary pointed to the edge of the clearing.

Aeneas smiled and she could see the warmth rise in his face as the narrow path opened. Mary wondered if he was thinking of Soman.

"When you have seen Soman, you will be able to open the path. Until then you will need to follow me," Aeneas instructed her.

"But I just saw the bear."

"You saw only what the spirit of the path allowed you to see. You have not yet seen Soman." Aeneas jumped into the forest and waved for Mary to follow. "Now follow me and stay close."

Mary followed and as she looked back, the forest closed in behind her. What did Aeneas mean about her not seeing the bear, and what did seeing a bear have to do with the magical creation of this path? Mary put those thoughts aside. She needed to find Max and somehow running this path would get her closer. That is all she needed to understand now. She picked up her pace as she heard the crackling of branches of the path closing in just behind her.

CHAPTER 29

In the Wasteland with Kytann

Max and Kytann walked for hours in the dark of the forest. Max's vision became accustomed to the shades of grey overlaying the field of black. The land that they walked through was a vast wasteland of moist earth and torn stumps. Max looked up and could not see what it was that separated him from the sun. As far as he knew he could just as well have been in a massive cave. After awhile each torn stump began to look like the last. Hours had passed without talking until the familiarity of boredom overtook Max and he spoke. "Have you always lived in the forest?"

Kytann looked back at him with mild contempt. "This desolate wasteland is where I have found peace from the war that will never end. But this is not my home." Kytann's red eyes showed a flicker of gold as his mind faded to better times.

"Where is it that you came from?" Max kicked a clod of dirt not thinking much of the question.

Kytann, also caught up in the monotony of the journey, looked down at Max, wondering how it had come to be that such a great creature as he was walking in a wasteland with a boy. "My home is in the spirit world where light abounds within golden halls and where great songs are sung on the voice of the wind."

Max stopped for a moment and looked at Kytann, not knowing what to think. "So why are you here in this dark place now, away from your home?"

Kytann kept walking as if in a dream world. "We were enslaved in the city of light. I had not seen it at first myself, but when I was shown what freedom was I felt suffocated by the light. He sought to rule over us, to dominate our every move. Our mind was not our own, my songs were not my own. Joy left me when I was shown the truth, but one of my own, a great mind, showed us a different way, a way that offered hope." Kytann's voice faded into a whisper.

"What was your hope?"

"There was no escape from the eyes of the King. He saw all. I could never be free from him until he was dead. It was such a simple solution to our problem." Kytann looked down at Max, his eyes wearied by many sleepless nights. "I wrote such beautiful music in those times. If I were able to sing them here these dark trees would burst out in song." A frown replaced his far off look. "But those days are now gone. Now all I have is darkness and war. We killed him and yet he lived. But there was a rumor within our ranks that a seed soaked in his dying blood could produce a weapon powerful enough to defeat him."

"To defeat who?"

"To defeat the bear who is not a bear." Kytann's head twitched left and right as he spoke.

Max backed away not knowing what to think.

"We will find the tree that I planted so many years ago and from it we will form for you an arrow. With that arrow we will finally kill the bear and with his death we will find freedom for your sister." Kytann controlled his twitching and his eyes glowed red.

CHAPTER 30

A Vision of Becky

Franz never woke up before John did, but this morning he made it a point to get up early. He had not talked to John about going on the path alone. In fact, he enjoyed being on the path with John so much that he had no real desire to take the path alone. He just wanted to know if he could do it.

He sneaked over to the edge of the wood and took a step toward a tree. The path spread as he let his foot fall on the familiar soft soil. He looked behind his shoulder. He would only be gone a moment, and with that thought he bounded into the path and the forest closed up behind him. The path was narrower without John, as if the path sensed it did not need to accommodate John's girth. As Franz took one more leap, the path opened up at the clearing from where he started. John was still sleeping on the grass. Franz looked behind him as the path closed in. He had only been on the path alone for seconds but had felt lonely during that brief time. There was no more reason to go into the forest alone. He had proven it could be done, and had done it. With that thought he took a great leap and landed on John's back waking him up in grand style. John laughed at the intrusion to his slumber. The two had a quick breakfast, both anxious to get back on the narrow path together.

Halfway into the morning it seemed that they had gone much deeper into the forest than the path would usually take them. Although there was always light above them as the path opened the trees above, the rest of the forest appeared darker and the stale smell on the path increased.

Franz followed close behind John, tunneling in and out of the main path, and as abruptly as they had begun their journey the path opened into a wide dark trail. Two wolves were caught unaware and without thinking John raised his halberd and let it fall, cleaving the first wolf's head from his shoulders. John did not slow down although in his mind everything seemed to be in slow motion, as if he was watching himself run through the damp trail. Franz followed close behind and threw one of his knives, killing the second wolf. He did not bother retrieving the knife, knowing that Soman would see that it was replaced in his belt in the morning if not sooner. The two reached the far wall of the dark trail and continued running as the narrow path opened up in front of them. They could hear howls of wolves in the distance, and the sounds seemed to be coming closer.

The next dark trail that they crossed was twice as wide as the previous one, and it had torn out stumps scattered across its breadth. Six wolves stood in a circle in front of them as they ran head on toward the pack. John remembered later thinking that it would have made more sense to veer off to one side or the other but he felt compelled to maintain the same line of the path from which he had emerged from the forest.

John raised his halberd and the wolves readied themselves to fight. John's halberd swooped a great arc, separating two heads from their owners. A third wolf bit into John's arm tearing flesh and drawing blood. Franz's knife plunged into the side of the wolf's head and he dropped to the ground. John and Franz kept up their pace staying in line with their path. John raised his halberd again and saw the next wolf in front of him. Unlike the others, he caught the look in the wolf's eyes before his next blow fell. Those eyes seemed sad. Was it because they knew that death had finally found their master or was it something deeper?

John took several more steps as the path opened at the far end of the wide trail and looked back at the dead wolves in their path. Two wolves were left alive, watching John and Franz disappearing into the forest. Their eyes glowed with hate, but behind the hate John thought he saw sadness, the same sadness that he had seen in the eyes of the wolf he had just killed. The remainder of the run was not as joyful as the morning's had been and John's mind questioned why the path had led them to kill some wolves but leave some behind and the necessity of it all.

That evening Soman shared their evening meal. John was quiet and was slow to eat. Soman was now eating cherries one at a time, as if each one was a precious gift to savor.

"What did you see on the path today, John?" Soman moved closer to the fire. He took a nearby stick and began poking it, looking into the fire. Embers swirled in the slight breeze and drifted up to the stars above.

"We crossed several of the wolf trails." John looked down at the scar on his arm where Soman had healed the bite of the wolf. "We killed several of the wolves."

"The path leads us to where we need to be." Soman continued to poke at the fire as if entranced by the glowing wood.

John picked up a stick and began doing the same. The fire was mesmerizing. "Your song creates all things, maintains all things. It controls the path." John stared into the fire. "I looked into the eyes of the wolves and saw a deep sadness. Was it right to kill them? Was it necessary?" John followed an ember now swirling round and round over a log caught in a tiny whirlwind. Under his breath he whispered for only himself to hear, "Was it necessary for Becky to die?"

"I sing the great song written by the Old One at the beginning of time, but the song does not control the path. There is a great Spirit that resides in you when your heart resides in me. At that moment you are in harmony with the great song and the Spirit opens the path. It is the Spirit that allows you to see me clearly when you are running in the path. To truly see me is to love me and to love me is to desire me above all else. It is me you are chasing as you run the narrow path, but it is the Spirit within you that creates the path that you run."

Soman began to hum a song and a light breeze blew into the fire, swirling the embers round and round. The logs glowed bright yellow and orange in the same circle as if the glow was chasing the embers above. "The Old One wrote the great song before the beginning of time, knowing all things to come. Each sorrow woven into that fabric has a purpose, sometimes known only to Him who wrote it. The narrow path can only be lived moment by moment. It was not designed to chase the sorrows of the past. The path lives only in the moment. It only moves forward." Soman looked up at John and saw that he was still staring into the fire and that his heart was still heavy. He then began to sing a song.

As John stared into the swirling fire he saw in the darkness of the fire Becky lying on her bed just before she died. But as the vision continued she did not die. John watched as she recovered from her sickness. After Becky had been returned to her full health John watched as the years passed by. Year after year they tried in vain to have children and the two became bitter and cold. John searched the corners of the vision looking for the great bear to be watching from the side but he was nowhere to be found. Decades passed and Becky's heart grew colder. John tried to turn away not able to bear the monster that she had become, a monster that he had helped to create, but there was no escape from the vision as it marched on. From deep inside he cried out for mercy and the vision returned to the younger Becky on her death bed from where the vision had began. Becky died in the peace of sleep as John had remembered and as the clouds of the vision receded John found himself staring across the fire, his vision blurred with the tears that filled his eyes.

Soman went to John and wiped away his tears with a furry paw. "Many things will come to pass in this life that you will not understand at their appointed time. Do you know where the narrow path is taking you as you run its length? You must trust that the path set before you is for your good, and although it may not always take you to where you want to go, it will always take you to where you need to be."

John looked at the scars on the great bear. He knew that many of those scars were from saving him from the wolves many nights ago and he trusted Soman. That night John lay awake staring at the stars, marveling at how vast the power of the Old One must be to have created all these things with a song. The last thing he thought as sleep overtook him was that it was a truly beautiful thing.

CHAPTER 31

Kytann's Songs

Max and Kytann had made camp near the base of a massive tree the previous night. Max awoke to the darkness that had sent him to sleep. They were now deep into the forest, still a half day's journey to Kytann's tree. Kytann lay still next to Max with his left eye half open. Max wondered whether the twitching fits that he had when he got mad had deformed the eye so that it could not shut when he slept. As if in answer to the thought, the giant's red eye turned toward him and Kytann arose without making any noise. Here the forest was completely quiet. There were no sounds of leaves rustling or small animals running about through the barren dirt that surrounded them.

"We are now entering the deep of the forest." Kytann only whispered, as if afraid of making even the slightest sound. "The tree that we seek is at the very center of the forest. It has been many hundreds of years since I have trod this desolate earth. The darkness of the deep forest has drawn the most vile of creatures that came to be when the earth was cursed. It was the curse that created them. They now hide here in the dark of the forest from the light above."

Max stepped on a small twig that crunched under his feet. The small sound seemed to echo in the silence of the dark. Kytann turned back toward him with his red eyes glaring. "It would be better not to wake those who sleep in the deep of the forest. I cannot guarantee your safe passage here. I cannot even guarantee my own."

Max followed close to Kytann, able only to see a few yards away from the wolf. He had not noticed it before but now that they were surrounded by total darkness the small white patch on the wolf's front paw seemed to glow as they walked. Other than the faint red glow from Kytann's eyes it was the only light for miles. Kytann noticed Max staring at his paw.

"Before we were thrown from the light, that was my color. Now it serves only to remind me of the slavery of my past, slavery to the light. There was not a moment of the day that our every action was not accounted for. For countless years we walked under the constant surveillance of the one whom we served, the one whom I shall not name. It seemed that there was no escape. To even consider separation from the light was folly. We were without hope until we were shown the truth. It was only then that we were made free." Kytann studied Max as they walked.

"What was the truth that set you free?"

"The farmer showed you the mechanical working of his house?"

Max nodded, thinking of the lost house for the first time since they had entered the forest.

"It was a clumsy model of reality, but it nevertheless revealed the essential truth that set us all free."

Yearning at the answer, Max looked at the great eye of Kytann. "I don't understand."

Kytann turned and looked at the boy but kept walking. He spoke with disdain. "It is small wonder. You are the child of man. The span of your years is but a blink of the eye to me. It is a wonder to me you can even talk. But since we have nothing else to do on this journey of ours I will explain it to you, so that before your pointless years on this earth have ended you will know the truth."

"At the very beginning, if there even was a very beginning, a great power created all that we see. My kind came into being after this wondrous event. The great enslaver, the bear who is not a bear …" A twitch escaped his controlled speech and Kytann paused before he continued talking. "He taught that all things became and were sustained by him. We all served him, praising him endlessly for the glorious existence that we found ourselves in. We each glorified him in our own way and mine was through song. The songs that I wrote were the most glorious works you could possibly imagine, so glorious I suspect you would explode if you were to ever fully experience one. But they were always about him, never about me. Why should I not sing a song glorifying the greatest songwriter that ever was? I wrestled with that question for thousands of years."

"What does 'glorifying' him mean?" Max looked up at Kytann who was now looking straight ahead.

"Do not trifle me with such questions, child of man. It is inconceivable that you will understand the wisdom passing through my lips as we walk. I tell you these things only for my own satisfaction. Now back to our glorious moment of insight. The greatest of us had been examining the universe in detail for millions of years. Whether it was created or not we could never say, but what was clear is that it was amazingly consistent. Consistent like the devices you call machines. It was so consistent that we could predict where the stars would be thousands of years in advance. I even wrote a song about the greatness of their predictability." Kytann looked down at Max imagining him exploding as he listened to the song. A smile crept on his face as he continued on.

"Where was this great power that had created the vast universe? Did it even exist? We did not even know if we had been created for we did not remember such a moment. All that we knew for sure was that the universe moved in predictable ways like a machine. It was then that it dawned on the greatest of us that no one was controlling the universe. It was operating on its own through set rules we called laws. We were free to set our own destiny. If the universe was truly a machine running on its own why should we give glory to anyone but ourselves? We only needed to free ourselves from the light." Kytann paused and twisted his head as if remembering a pain inflicted long ago.

"Freeing ourselves from the light turned out to be more difficult than we had anticipated. There was a great war, a war that still rages today where we are still fighting for our freedom to glorify ourselves as we see fit. He who enslaved us had a magical power over the machine that was the universe and drove us with this magic to the darkness of this world. For years we lived under the threat of total destruction when the unthinkable happened. He who had enslaved us came down to this world in the form of a mere man. It seemed too good to be true. I wrote a song of it and if you live through this short adventure of ours I will share it with you and we will see if you will explode in ecstasy."

Max looked up to Kytann not knowing if he was serious or not. Kytann showed no signs of joking. "What did you do then?"

"We killed him, of course." Kytann looked out into the darkness, his mind in another time.

"So aren't you free now?"

"I do not expect you to understand the complexities that followed. It was hard for even me to understand why our hard earned freedom did not find us in that hour. But it did not. For three days we celebrated, killing many in our joy, which was the custom at the time."

Max gave Kytann a wary look.

"Do not judge me, child of man. Besides, I only kill now when my solitude is threatened. The joy of killing has fled from me, leaving only boredom. Where was I? Oh yes … three days. We had peace for three days. Three days out of an eternity. I doubt you can conceive of how short a time that really represents. Three days after we had killed him who had kept us in slavery he rose from the dead and unleashed a power on the earth that has forced many of us into the darker areas of the world. To roam in the light is to invite his wrath. It was fortunate that I had a contingency plan. When he was just a boy I acquired six drops of his blood and soaked six special seeds, knowing that they would absorb his magic. I then planted them in the far corners of the world. The tree that we now seek is from the first seed that I planted. It is why I made my home here in the forest, to be close to the magic of the tree and wait for the opportunity to end what we had begun so long ago. Once we are done I will write a glorious song telling of how we killed the bear who is not a bear. If you live through this quest I may even mention you in the song. But knowing the bear as I do, I think that is unlikely."

CHAPTER 32

Soman and Franz

Soman awoke in the quiet of the morning. Franz was next to him sharing his warmth, and John was curled up on the other side of the clearing. The river quietly rumbled to his side, the first lights of dawn painting the water pink. Soman quietly walked to the water, took a drink and sat by its edge. He looked up to the sunrise and gave thanks for all that he had been given and for all that he would have today. Each day was a wonderful adventure, some pain mixed in for good measure, that to be sure. He looked down at the scars that covered his body. He had known a measure of pain. Where would the path take him today? It was always a mystery, and yet not. He had explained to John in the past that even though he sang the song that sustained the world, he did not direct the path. The Great Spirit directed the path in accordance to a portion of the song that had not yet been sung. It was beautiful to contemplate.

A sliver of light lit the middle of the river flashing bright in his eyes. It was time to go, the path beckoned. Soman went back to Franz and quietly woke him up. "It is time to go find your brother and sister."

Franz wiped the sleep from his eyes and looked toward John.

"John's path will be different than ours for a time, but we will see him again."

Soman nudged Franz near the stream and waded in. Once he was floating on his back he pulled Franz aboard on his soft belly. The river picked up speed as they veered to its center.

* * * * *

Franz looked back at John still asleep as he passed out of view. He pulled his hair back and looked down the river wondering what the path would bring today. He ran his fingers through Soman's thick belly fur and took a deep breath of air that was still cool enough to chill. Once on the path, it seemed to have a life of its own. You never knew what you would find, so Franz kept his eyes open tracking the river's edge, one hand on a knife in his belt.

CHAPTER 33

Mary's Sword

It was midday and Mary was drenched in sweat. She had been running the narrow path with Aeneas for hours. The path opened into a twenty yard circular opening. Once Mary was in the opening she bent down and grabbed her knees to catch her breath. She looked back as the forest closed the path behind them. The opening was lined with bushes adorned with blackberries and raspberries. Aeneas sat down next to one of the bushes and began to eat.

Mary stayed standing near where they came out of the forest. She took a step toward the trees but the path did not open. "I don't understand. I am thinking of the bear in my mind. I can picture him clearly. I believe in the path. Why will it not open for me?"

Aeneas sat patting the ground next to him. Mary sighed, walked over to the spot, and sat down.

Aeneas sat with his broad sword in his lap, running one hand over it as he ate with the other. The metal was different than any Mary had seen before. It glittered in the sunlight like it was on fire sending spots of colored light dancing all around them. Mary's mood was soon revived and she began to eat.

"It is not an understanding of the path or a picture of Soman in your mind that opens the path. It is not a magical thing to be manipulated by your will." Aeneas took a portion of his cloak and polished an inscription on the blade of the sword.

"Then how can I learn to open the path?" Frustrated, Mary threw a berry to the other side of the clearing.

"You cannot learn to open the path. No one can." Aeneas walked over to pick up the berry that Mary had thrown. He brought it back rolling it between his fingers, studying it as if to look for some secret hidden in the creases of the fruit. "The berries are good, would you agree?"

Mary looked back at him with a mouth full of blackberries and nodded.

"Do you remember when you first chose to desire such a berry? Was it a difficult choice, I wonder?"

Mary looked at Aeneas as if he were mad. "No one chooses to like berries, you either do or you don't."

"Yes, that is true. Sadly, we do not choose our own desires." Aeneas grabbed another berry from the bush next to him, studied it, and then ate it. "I am wondering what you thought of the great bear?"

Mary gave a thoughtful look wondering where this conversation was going. "He looked dangerous, dangerous and odd, very odd. A talking bear is very odd." Mary paused as she thought back to the encounter. "Although there was something special about him, almost royal, for lack of a better word."

"Beauty is an odd thing, abhorring definition like a wild animal would a cage. It is a reflection of our desires. The great bear is the most beautiful thing I can imagine. I harbor within me a desire to be with him beyond what rational thought can explain. I do not choose to desire him because I understand something that you do not. The desire of the bear was a gift to me."

Aeneas stood up and handed his sword to Mary. "Have you ever handled a blade such as this?"

Mary took the sword in her hands. It was lighter than she would have guessed. She held the sword out in front of her, feeling its weight as she watched it sparkle in the sun. The grip of the sword was made of a dark wood and felt very cold to the touch.

"I have never held a sword before. It is like holding a feather."

Aeneas smiled. "There are none others like it." He walked to the edge of the forest and taking a small knife from his belt he cut a young limb from the tree in front of him. He trimmed the branch into a bare pole and swung it in front of him as if testing a new sword.

After an hour's time showing Mary the basics of sword play he squared himself in front of Mary holding the stick at guard. "Hit me if you can."

Mary smiled, "the blade will run right through your pole and into you."

Aeneas raised the pole and swung it down at Mary's thigh.

Mary shifted the sword without thinking and diverted the blow. She looked down at the pole. It did not have so much as a nick from where the sword had hit it. "This sword is light but you have let it run dull, it could not cut even a leaf."

"That is true, but it was not designed to cut leaves." Aeneas turned and swung his pole full force at Mary's head.

Mary saw the move too late to move on her own, but the sword, still in her hands, found its way up to parry the blow. Mary's eyes grew wide as the pole hit her sword inches away from her face.

"You are close to finding the path. The sword will only protect the pure of heart." Aeneas raised his pole again, turning as he moved, and brought the pole down low toward Mary's knee. Again the sword found its way down to block the blow.

Aeneas continued to attack as the afternoon wore on. Mary became more comfortable with the sword, her muscle memory conforming to where the sword directed her to go. After an hour her mind began to wander as her body continued on with its learning. She looked at Aeneas and thought about how different things were now than when they had lived in the church with him. Then things had been calm and he had talked about the things that priests talk about. He had taught them the story of the gospel as he had the rest of the villagers. Mary had always accepted what was said but it had never really factored into her life. It was history and therefore dry and without meaning. The stained glass windows were different, though. She walked them many times in the early morning waiting for the boys to awake. The man who had died on the cross seemed so real, and so sad. She imagined what his life must have been like. The stories of his life filtered into her mind as if Aeneas were retelling each one. His life really was beautiful, beautiful and sad, like the stained glass windows that depicted it.

Mary's mind wandered along the corridor of distant memories, following a path deeper and deeper into her own heart, until she finally reached a musty old door at the end of the path that she had never opened. She opened the door, fearing the filth that lay beyond. Passing through the door she waded through the grime and filth that lay within and found something that she did not remember placing there, something so beautiful that she would never have left it in the dark realms of her heart. Without thinking she grabbed at that which was beautiful and let loose of the filth that lay around it. With that she felt a heavy blow deflected from the sword.

Aeneas picked up the intensity of the attack. Mary's sword kept pace but she was forced to back up to keep her footing. Harder and harder Aeneas fought, keeping Mary in a faster and faster retreat. She reached the tree line without knowing it, continuing to back up to maintain her defense. Without realizing what was happening she had backed into the narrow path. The two were totally engulfed by trees before she understood where she was. Before she had time to contemplate what had just happened Aeneas yelled for her to turn and run. Without thinking she took off and the path moved forward.

Mary ran, her mind filled with the confusion of the moment and the thought of the beauty that had been placed in her dark heart, a beauty that she knew the great bear had left there. As she thought of the great bear she saw him through this newfound beauty, which now seemed obvious. As she ran she thought it odd she had not noticed it before. She now chased his image through the forest wanting nothing more than to know more about him, to be with him, to enjoy him. She ran fast, very fast.

* * * * *

Aeneas kept up as he must, or he would be left in the crushing trees that closed in behind them. Aeneas saw the path opening up in front of them and was thankful for the promise of rest. As they exited the forest they came to a dark open plain. Aeneas looked back at the tree line for a weapon but saw none and then nodded to himself, having known this time would come sooner or later. He had thought it would be later, but that was part of the beauty of the path. It always kept you guessing, kept fueling the adventure from one moment to the next. It would be good to have a break. He smiled as the thought soaked in. Good indeed.

"You are now a path runner," he told Mary, "but the path does not end at the tree line. We are always on the path, even now. Keep your sword at the ready. You will soon find out what it was designed to cut."

CHAPTER 34

Something Worse Than Worms

They had walked for what seemed to be hours before Kytann came to a stop. He looked down at Max without saying a word and motioned with his head to the darkness that lay in front of him.

Max strained to look ahead to see what looked like a massive black pillar that reached to the sky. Its width was at least thirty feet, and no branches could be seen from where they stood. Kytann began to approach the enormous tree as if he were stalking it and Max followed close behind not making a sound. As they neared the tree the ground grew warm as if the earth itself was angry with what lay within it. The bleached bones of wild beasts both large and small lay strewn around the tree. As Kytann's white paw landed near one of the skeletons Max noted a deformed look to its skull as if the bone itself had been melting as the beast had died. Its eye teeth were long, no less than a hand's length. They were now contorted and twisted as if they had tried to escape the tormented animal before their fate was sealed in the dark earth in which they now lay.

When they reached the tree Max went to lay his hand on it but Kytann swatted his hand away before he could touch it. Kytann then spoke as a voice within his mind, "Do not touch the bark of the black tree or you will suffer the fate of those we just passed."

Max looked up silently as Kytann frowned and nodded his head. Kytann then drew one of his razor sharp claws into the side of the tree, cutting deep into the wood. The claw made a hissing sound as it sliced into the black tree and the stale air was filled with the smell of singed hair. Kytann pulled his claw away from the wood with half of its length burned off. Kytann grimaced, then smiled as he took his white paw and again sliced into the tree's flesh, carving out a sliver of black wood that fell to the hard earth with a thud.

Kytann looked over his shoulder as if spooked by a noise in the distance. With a renewed haste he held the wood down with one paw and carved out ten arrows with the claw of the other. The arrows needed no metal tip or feathered ends when he was finished, their form complete as he carved each one. His claws no longer smoked when he touched the wood and without having to be careful about burning himself he quickened his pace. With a skill a thousand years in the making he carved out a solitary bow in the remaining wood.

Looking behind him again he motioned for Max to pick up the bow and the arrows he had made. The wood was light and cool to the touch, cooler than what it should have been, especially after lying on the hot earth near the tree. As Max's fingers ran through the soil he could feel the dirt vibrating. He ran his hand over the bow, feeling its strength. The wood was as smooth as ice. Kytann then bent low, rubbing one of his whiskers across Max's face. Max understood and pulled on the whisker with all his might. It held tight until Kytann jerked away, and Max rolled into the darkness holding the whisker. Lying on the ground Max could now hear the sound of something approaching, of many things approaching. The small vibration that he had felt earlier now visibly shook the ground.

The voice in his head boomed. "We are running out of time, string the bow now!" Kytann now stood over him and rolled his head as if hurrying him on. Max took the bow and strung it with the whisker from Kytann. Carrying the arrows now in his quiver, he looked out into the darkness from whence they had come.

Kytann held up his white paw toward the dark and the fur appeared to glow, casting a dim light onto the dark field. In the distance they could see the very earth shaking as if in a fit of rage. Then suddenly monstrous worms one to two feet in girth erupted from the shaking soil. As they turned toward Max they opened their slime covered mouths to reveal rows and rows of razor teeth that gleamed even in the dim light. Hundreds of these creatures now slithered over the dark plains, but kept their distance from the tree itself. The voice in Max's head again beckoned, "Climb upon my back and do not waste an arrow on these lowly creatures. We will need every arrow."

Kytann bent down and Max climbed upon his back. He stood twice the height of a horse and was wide enough that Max had to grab onto his neck hair so that he would not slide off. Kytann lowered himself down, making ready to sprint into the field of worms. He then let out a bloodcurdling howl. Every muscle in Max's body contracted and froze at the sound. It was then that Kytann leaped forward toward the worms. Max could not move at all, not even his head, as they charged through the slime. Had he not already grabbed Kytann's hair he would have surely fallen off. At first he thought it odd that none of the worms were attacking; they just seemed limp on the earth. It then occurred to him that they were frozen by Kytann's howl, just as he was. Kytann covered thirty yards with each bound. Max could feel the softened impact when Kytann landed on one of the worms. They were several bounds away from clearing the worms when Max turned his head and looked down on a worm they had just crushed. It lay in slimy ruin, some of which was sticking to Kytann's white paw. Max could feel himself regaining control of his body and he leaned down into Kytann's back as a worm sprang out of the twisting slimy mess below. The worm meant to swallow Max whole and just barely missed. Kytann now bounded left and right, evading as many of the sharp teeth as he could as they made it out of the worms' lair.

As Kytann finally landed on firm ground the earth seemed to shake, much more than what Max would have anticipated from Kytann's weight. Kytann now spoke with an audible voice. "Ready your bow, child of man, the worms are not the worst thing we shall find in the deep darkness of the forest."

The earth shook again and Max pulled an arrow from his quiver but saw nothing. Then from the corner of his eye he saw a great hand the size of Kytann reaching down to grab him. Kytann veered suddenly to the right and the white of his paw glowed bright. The hand retreated, covering the eyes of a massive giant that Max could now make out.

"Shoot it now, while it is blinded!" Kytann bellowed.

Max drew back a black arrow and let it fly. The arrow seemed to pick up speed as it flew into the chest of the monstrous beast. It gave out a deafening cry of pain as the flesh around where the arrow pierced burst into flame and then ash as the hole widened.

"Again, hit it again!" Kytann veered as the angry beast swung down with a tree trunk he had clasped in his other hand.

Max could feel the breeze from the near miss and reloaded. Another arrow flew this time into the monster's knee. A wail more frightening than Kytann's howl erupted from the giant, a string of noises that Max did not understand.

Kytann laughed as the beast fell forward into the field of worms. "It was cursing in an ancient tongue, Max, called *Latin*. He is one of three left of a Roman legion that trespassed the darkness of the forest long ago. The power of the dark tree made him into the monster that you saw. Hold fast to those arrows, his brothers may be nearby."

Kytann ran like the wind through the dark of the field that night and they did not stop until the trees of the forest could again be seen.

CHAPTER 35

The Mist

Aeneas kept a quick pace with Mary as they made their way through the dark plain. The trees were few and far between. They would offer no shelter if the wolves found them. He would have preferred to steer clear of wolf track in this place, but the soil told a story of many wolves crossing in all directions, some very recently. He watched Mary as they walked. She carried the sword with such familiarity that a stranger might guess she had been born with it. It lay upon her shoulder as if seeking a good vantage point to spy out the enemy that lurked close by. It was odd to believe that a sword could think, but Aeneas knew that this one did.

Or rather he who controlled it did. He had wielded that blade for thirty years. For thirty years he had been in the service of the bear. He looked down at his arms, more scar than flesh. He had squeezed out every ounce of service his old body had to offer. Had it not been for the strength of the blade the wolves would have taken him ten years prior. He stretched his fingers and then regripped his staff. His swollen joints cracked as if to plead with him to let them be. Have peace, old body, he told himself. Soon you will have your rest.

"There is a high point in the distance." Aeneas pointed his staff straight ahead. "Let us go there so that we can at least know the lay of the land."

"There are many wolf tracks here." Mary's voice carried with it more than a hint of concern.

"We must trust in the bear and trust in the path." Aeneas brought his staff down and used it to help him walk. His legs ached from the morning run. He reached down to rub his thigh. It was unusual for him to ache so and he felt for any cuts or rips that he may not have noticed before. As he raised his head back up he saw the glimmer of the sword. It was then that he realized that the strength of the sword was leaving him. Its master had not changed, but the one wielding it had. He smiled, knowing the sword had chosen the next path runner well. And to think all this time he had thought the sword would be passed on to John. He was such a huge man, the choice had seemed obvious to him. But then, he was not such an obvious choice, either. Aeneas looked back at the sword nostalgically and saw the glimmer of yellow specks in its metal. It would flicker like that in a starry night, but it was only late afternoon and the sky was covered with darkness in the plain. Aeneas looked around him and saw specks of yellow glowing in the darkness behind them like fireflies. He nudged Mary on her shoulder to quicken the pace. "We have company behind us. We need to make for that high land. It looks like the only defensible position within reach."

Mary looked behind and then broke into a slow jog. The bouncing yellow flecks matched her pace but did not close the gap, seemingly happy to keep the intruders on their present course.

"Their numbers are growing," Aeneas told her. "I have never seen so many wolves. There must be at least a hundred." Mary was now running toward a path that led to the high point.

Aeneas did what he could to keep up. "The path has led us to their den. There is a great wolf that lives in the darkness. Let us hope that we do not find him."

Mary now found herself up against a rock cliff that the path ran against. The path climbed up and she could see the high point fifty yards ahead. It was then that the wolves closed their distance, the whites of their teeth plainly in view.

We have been herded into this spot, Mary realized. She looked all around her. The wolves circled them, weaving in and out around each other. With the rock wall to their back Mary pointed the sword out toward them and they shrank back for a moment having seen the sword before. Then the pack converged and the air was filled with the killing howl of the wolves.

Mary raised the sword and let it arc down low. The blade gleamed with joy as it beheaded four wolves in one blow. Mary then brought it down in a figure eight, and four more heads fell. The ground nearby grew slick from the blood that spilled freely.

Aeneas swung the staff hard around him protecting Mary's flank. He no longer had the sword to guide him but his muscles had been well trained by years of guidance from the weapon. A wolf's skull cracked as the staff hit it from the side, creating a gruesome sound that moved the wolves back a step as they sized up their two prey. That was all the room Aeneas needed as he nudged Mary up the path.

The pack now sent in only two or three at a time, testing their capacity, and the sword took as many heads as were given to it. Aeneas held the rest of the pack off Mary's back with his staff as they climbed the path. His joints, now occupied with wielding the staff, seemed to have forgotten their previous grievances and he churned the staff left and right, breaking bone and smashing skull.

Mary caught site of Aeneas out of the corner of her eye and wondered at the sight. One blow to a wolf landed so hard that it threw the wolf down the path bowling over three others that were just behind. "We are nearly to the top. I think I hear water."

Mary swung the sword in front of them, killing three wolves. The path was now clear and they sped up the path. Once they reached the top they saw why the wolves were so happy to keep them moving up the path. To their left was a cliff, and from the sound of it, the rough water of a river far below. Mary looked over the cliff and saw only a dense mist that filled the chasm. To their right was a massive cave. Mary looked at the tracks leading out of the cave and her knees gave way for a moment. Aeneas, now back to back with her, kept her up. The tracks were those of a wolf, but a monster of a wolf. From within the cave a low growl could be heard, which grew with every passing moment into a cacophony of howls. From Kytann's cave emerged the rest of the pack.

Wolves attacked from the path and the cave. Their strategy seemed almost suicidal as they rushed toward the two and were slain by the dozen. The sword now moved so fast that it whistled through the air singing a song of justice long delayed but now executed in full force. One of the wolves hurdled Aeneas and sailed over Mary, dragging his claws over her right shoulder and ripping flesh down to bone. She continued to fight, killing wolves blow after blow, but it now was only a matter of time. Seeing that the strategy had worked, wolves now were coming from the air from all directions. Most flew by over the cliff disappearing into the mist and the raging water that it hid.

"Your path is through the mist, Mary. You must jump." Aeneas had his back to Mary, swinging his staff one way and then another and prodding the wolves back in a semicircle around them.

Mary looked down into the mist. She heard the raging water of the river crashing against the rocks far below. "If I jump into that I will surely die."

"You must trust in the path, trust in the bear." She heard fatigue in Aeneas' voice. Each word separated with a gasp for more air.

"I do not know the bear. How can I trust him to save me through that?" Mary's blade stopped swinging as she stared down into the mist, seemingly oblivious to the wolves that continued to attack.

As if jolted with electricity, Aeneas swung his staff with the force of ten men, sending wolves flying into the growing pack that surrounded him, clearing a perimeter between them and the wolves. He now spared one look back at her. "You are a path runner now. But to stay on the path you must trust in the great bear. But for now, trust in me, and jump."

Mary looked into Aeneas' eyes seeing both the fire of a great warrior and the exhaustion of an old man. She then turned toward the mist and jumped.

Aeneas saw her disappear into the darkness below and smiled, knowing that trust in him would not be enough to send Mary into the abyss. He then turned back toward the wolves. Many were hunching down, making ready to follow Mary below through the mist and wreak whatever havoc they could in the fall. Aeneas lowered his head and with what strength was left with him charged into the pack sending the front line of wolves flailing into a confused mass of fang and claw. Aeneas had known when he entered the dark land that his path would end here. His eyes shone with fire as he raised his staff and killed one last demon wolf, using the last ounce of energy his body had left to give. It took only moments for the surrounding wolves to tear into his flesh, but he seemed to feel no pain at that point. His last thought as he passed out of the darkness of the forest was one word ... beautiful.

CHAPTER 36

Running Alone Yet Not Alone

John looked up at the sun. The warmth felt good on his face. He had awakened alone that morning. At first he thought Soman had taken Franz out for a short run, but an hour passed and he was still alone. He had decided to take the narrow path to find them but the path had only taken him five minutes into the forest and then led him back to their camp. He had taken the path four times, each time returning from where he had started. Once he resolved that he was not going anywhere this morning, he sat down and ate berries while listening to the sounds of the forest. At first his mind raced with thoughts of why he was left alone, and then he began to worry that Soman and Franz might be in trouble. But after an hour of sitting in the quiet of the forest his mind wandered to the sky and he noticed a bird flying high above. The bird seemed happy as it made giant circles in the blue sky. John wondered what it would be like to be the bird, flying high above the forest, worried about nothing other than the next turn it would take high above.

How many days had he been out in the forest with Soman? He had lost track of time in the dense forest. Each day was its own adventure, but the days ran together. What was it that tied them together? He ate another berry as he watched the bird above. It was the running … running with Soman. It was rhythmic. There was something relaxing and yet exerting about following the great bear on the path. Even when Soman was not with him and Franz in the flesh, he was with them. The bear was always on John's mind.

John got up and looked at the tree line. The worries of the morning had left him. He had no agenda. He missed running with the bear. That was all that he felt. With that thought he opened the path and began to run. The worries he left to the morning dew. As he ran he noticed how the bark of the trees circled in a shallow spiral, which almost gave the appearance of the trees dancing as he passed them by. As the afternoon passed the grass in the path grew longer, sometimes almost knee high, and he could see flowers, mostly red posies, along the sides of the path.

John ran for hours that afternoon and only stopped when the path led him back to their camp at the river at dusk. He caught several fish as Soman had taught him and cooked them over the fire. He looked into the fire thinking of running with the great bear. There was no one else at the fire but he knew he was not alone. He slept well that night looking forward to the next day's run. What would he find on the path tomorrow? It was all an adventure now. What would he find?

CHAPTER 37

Falling Through Darkness

Cool mist rushed against her face as Mary fell headlong into the dark. The blood from the wolves that covered her body loosened its grip on her skin as the mist poured over her, faster and faster, washing away the filth that enveloped her. Falling through the cool dark she lost all sense of thought, even fear, holding tight with both hands to the sword that had saved her in the den of wolves. The sound of water rushing over rock that had been a distant murmur grew into a deafening roar as she descended. The first thought that broke into her mind toward the end of the fall was that death was near. So be it, she thought. Aeneas had certainly found death up above on the cliff. Soon she would join him. With that thought she plunged into a deep froth of ice cold water. She sank and turned and was rolled by the cold water that seemed to attack from every side. Her muscles braced as she anticipated hitting rock, and like a rock she tumbled through the raging waters, the sword still tight in her grasp. Had she known how to swim she would have dropped the sword and made for the surface, but tumbling through the water she did not even know which direction was up.

It was at the height of her disorientation that a small hand grabbed under her arm and pulled her aboard a warm furry raft making its way down the rapids. Mary's first sight as she emerged from the cleansing waters was Soman smiling at her as she clung to the side of his massive body.

"Climb aboard my body, Mary, and together we shall ride through the path that lies ahead." Soman rolled slightly to one side, pulling Mary, who clung tight to his side, out of the water.

Mary crawled to the high point of the great bear's belly, where she found Franz standing, hands on hips, smiling down on her as if she were a stowaway on the ship that he captained. Mary froze for a moment, not believing what she saw. She had half given up hope of ever seeing Franz again, and yet there he stood with his wild hair matted down by the waters of the river like the mane of a small lion. Mary lifted herself to her knees and Franz ran into her embrace and their tears mixed with the waters of the river.

After gathering her senses she looked back into the darkness from whence she had come. "We must go back to save Aeneas. He is alone and surrounded by wolves."

"I saved Aeneas many years ago. The den is where his path on this earth ended." Soman let the water rushing by his face clear a tear from his eye. "The pain of this world is now behind him. He now runs on paths bathed by light, until the paths of this world have been remade."

Mary stretched her neck over the horizon of the great bear's girth to see the face of Soman. "The narrow path only moves forward, Mary, and we have much to do. John and Max will need our help soon."

Mary stared at Soman, not understanding. She smiled seeing the beauty and truth in his face, and she trusted him. She knew deep within that he was the one who had allowed her to leap into the darkness. She gripped her sword tight as she turned her head toward the river in front of them. The adventure had overtaken her. There was no turning back now. She was all in.

CHAPTER 38

The Following Day

Max rubbed his arms and legs, trying to stay warm as they journeyed back to Kytann's home. They were taking a short cut through a greener part of the forest. Max could feel the warmth of the sun when it peaked through the canopy above. He would slow his pace to stay in the sun when he could but Kytann kept them moving, nervous of what lurked in the sunny forest. It would take them a full day to make it back, he had said, and if you can't keep up you will be left behind.

Max looked over to Kytann walking next to him. He knew that he was being used to serve what Kytann thought was a greater end, but still he could not help but to feel some camaraderie with the beast that had saved his life near the tree.

* * * * *

"I am not a beast," Kytann said, disdain dripping from every word. He felt the affection emanating from Max. In days long past he would have used those emotions to wring out every ounce of service from the boy. But he was tired now, not just from the journey but from the world. And so mired in his apathy toward Max, he allowed himself the faintest warmth from the boy's affection.

Max's mind wandered back to their escape from the monsters in the dark. "What were those things on the plain of the dark tree?"

"The giant worms were once normal earth worms that tunneled the soil, now distorted and malformed from the dark magic of the tree. As for the giant men, that is a long story." Kytann now looked far off in the distance, thinking back to brighter days.

"How did the tree come to be?"

Kytann turned to look at Max while still walking as if judging whether he wanted to get into the matter. It was, to a certain extent, his own private affair. But still the journey today would be long and Max would certainly not survive the attack on the bear. Kytann looked back to where they were heading and began to speak.

"As I had noted before, if you had been listening, the cursed one to whom we were enslaved for countless eons chose for reasons known only to himself to enter into this world as a child of man. Once we were aware of this tactical blunder, we, of course, set out to kill him. Easier said than done. Although the lowly humans that surrounded him and governed over the area had unfettered access to him, hordes of beings such as myself, still loyal to his slavish will, guarded him night and day. We then tried working through the lowly humans to kill the child but he was swept off to an ancient land far away.

"Many of my kind gave up hope, but I followed him to that land. His magic was strong, and thus, it only seemed reasonable that the only way we would defeat him was through his own magic. That was quite a trick, since we had no access to him and did not understand how the magic worked." Kytann smiled in self satisfaction.

"It was I alone who devised a plan to steal the magic. I commanded six small insects to steal a single drop of blood from the body of our enslaver, reasoning correctly that the magic resided within his blood. I then placed each drop of blood within six tree seeds and went to every corner of the earth to plant the seeds, the first of which was planted here.

"The trees grew almost overnight. By the time I had made it back to the first tree that I had planted it was very similar to how you saw it yesterday. The magic from the tree infected all things around it and attracted darker things in this world that would have better been left out of my forest. It was the first time that I tried to harvest wood from the tree to kill our enslaver that I discovered the worms." Kytann held up his dark forepaw, showing old scars crisscrossing all along the hard hide under the gleaming black fur.

"They almost killed me. In fact, it was then that I first understood that the things of this world could conceivably kill me. It was a disturbing revelation as you might imagine. But then you, a son of man, are so easily killed it would be impossible for you to understand the change it had on me. I was more cautious from then on. I tried for years to get close to the black tree, but the worms and things worse than the worms guarded it closely as if the earth itself knew my plan and was angry with me. It is a preposterous thought, I know, but I was distraught at the time, and perhaps not thinking as clearly as I do today.

"I went in search for the other trees that I had planted, hoping to find a way to get a piece of just one so that I could fashion a weapon that would kill our enemy, but they were nowhere to be found. Then it came to me that although I could not safely approach the dark tree, perhaps a human could. Men were allowed to approach the enemy freely in this world. Perhaps the magic was not as strong against them in this world. Fortunately I had developed strong ties to the Roman throne. I arranged for thousands of soldiers to be deployed in Germania to quell a rebellion and expand the empire's domain, all for the glory of Rome.

"From that army I had first sent only a few men into the dark forest to fetch my wood. That did not go well. A beast of which I shall not now speak devoured them as they made it across the plain. I then sent hundreds of the soldiers hoping to overwhelm the beast, but sadly they were unsuccessful. Over the years I have sent thousands of soldiers into that killing field, and only three survived. They had not made it to the tree; their retreat had been cut off by the dark things that made their home in that place. And there they slowly changed into the animals that they once fought.

"That, Max, is the source of your giants. They are what have become of the three soldiers that were left behind. For years I had devised plan after plan to access the tree. And then the unthinkable happened. The same soldiers that I had used to get to the black tree killed him who I shall not name without any magic at all. I was, of course, elated, but at the same time somewhat frustrated that I had wasted all this time growing and trying to harvest the magical wood. As I noted earlier, these happy times were short-lived and since that time I have hidden in the forest waiting for a time to have my revenge.

"That is why you were such a fortunate find, Max. The soldiers were bent to my will, but you are a neutral. It was your heart that led us in close to the tree. Had I only known that back then, it would have saved me much grief. As it turns out, magic *will* be needed to kill the enemy. We will now finish what I started so many years ago."

CHAPTER 39

A Change of Plans

When Kytann and Max arrived near Kytann's lair the area was strangely silent. They made their way to the path that led to his cave and found the soil still damp with the blood from the day before. Kytann could smell the carnage of his wolves and ran like the wind up to the entrance of the cave where he found more than a hundred dead wolves strewn in front of it. The bones of the brown ghost that had evaded him for thirty years now lay piled at the entrance of the cave along with shreds of the brown cloak that he wore. The staff that had crushed many of his minions lay against the entrance of the cave.

The dozen wolves that still lived emerged from the cave once they heard their master return. Kytann looked back to the staff. The message was clear. He could no longer hide. The bear knew where he lived. He would have to attack or fall to the same fate as the wolves that now lay strewn upon the hill top.

The remaining wolves told him what had happened and of the girl diving over the cliff. He walked over to the cliff and looked down into the mist below. He had walked the side of the river before and knew what lay unseen. She could not have survived the fall. He then turned to Max, formulating what he would tell him.

"The bear has enslaved your sister with his mind. We must move now or she will be forever lost."

Anguish overtook Max. "We must save her. What must we do?"

"We must risk daylight in the trails where the forest is still green. The bear's servant of death can no longer hunt us. The bear himself will need to show himself in the open ... and we will be waiting."

CHAPTER 40

The Bait

John awoke from a deep sleep, his body alive with energy from the moment he opened his eyes. He grabbed a handful of berries and looked to the halberd lying against the far tree line. It seemed as if it had grown over the night, the staff longer, the ax blade wider. It looked anxious to be used. Not knowing what drove him with such energy this morning, he ran to the weapon and grasped it with both hands. Weighing it in his arms he smiled as he took his first step into the forest. The long grass and flowers of the prior run were gone. The path gave him soft loose soil to plant his feet on as he moved onward, the halberd at the ready over his shoulder. The forest was still this morning. No sounds could be heard in the quiet of the path. It was as if the forest itself had held its breath in anticipation of a long awaited reprieve from the darkness that infected its borders. John ran on, the joy from the day prior still burning strong in his heart.

* * * * *

That morning Max and Kytann lay in wait in a wide trail thirty yards from a crossroads. In the middle of the crossroads stood the last of Kytann's twelve wolves, nervously weaving in and out of each other, circles within circles.

Kytann looked down at Max. "The great bear will emerge from the dense forest and attack what is left of my wolves. You will have a clear view of him. You must hit him with the first shot. We may only have one chance. If he senses we have the means to kill him with the black arrows he will disappear into the forest and it may be centuries before I get another chance."

Max nodded and the two waited. Hours passed and the noon sun shone through the trees. Kytann's fur shone bright in the light, sparkling like a black diamond. Max looked up to Kytann wondering whether the bear was going to show.

Kytann looked down at Max. "He will show, be patient, I have waited an earth's age for this moment. You can wait a few more hours."

Max's mind drifted back to their walk from the dark field. "You mentioned there were other animals in the dark created by an ancient curse. What did you mean?"

Kytann looked down at Max, making eye contact. "Keep your mind sharp and your eye on the crossroads."

Several minutes passed, and Kytann again looked down. Max was at the ready, his focus solely on the wolves that circled ahead. He would have made a good centurion, Kytann thought. He then began to speak.

"Unlike my kind, your kind had a beginning. The bear who is not a bear created your kind from the substance of this world. He saw something in your kind to be invaluable. This was after we had been thrown from the light and we had figured out that something so valuable would be worth controlling. It was then that we showed the first of your kind the truth, albeit in a more simplified form than what we understood. They chose not to be slaves to the will of the enemy. What happened thereafter we could not have imagined.

"Your kind was sentenced to work a thistled earth and eventually die and return to the dirt from which you were made. It seemed reasonable and for the most part was what we expected. What followed was horrific. The enemy used his magic to curse the entire universe. We have borne the brunt of this retaliation since. The curse was not limited to a few weeds in the fields of men. There were things that were born into the world that day that live in the darkest places imaginable. They are monstrous and brutish with no reasoning capacity, only a lust to feed … to feed on us. A few men have fallen to these monsters, but men seldom tread in the darkest parts of the world.

"I did not account for these creatures when I planted the seeds. Who could have foreseen that the trees could become so powerful and dark?

The darkness of the trees attracts these beasts. They now have made their dwellings close to the dark tree, effectively guarding it. There is one that we did not see when we went to the tree that I think has developed a taste for man flesh. It moves like a shadow in the darkness, faster even than me. These things are terrible eating machines."

Kytann now gazed off, remembering events long past. "At the height of my quest I had brought over a thousand men to where we were, Max. They had war machines that threw fire and great spears. We lit the dark plain up with burning tar and oil and stormed the tree. The monsters from the deep erupted out of the holes on the far side of the dark tree. We ran them through with the giant spears and set them ablaze with fiery tar, but they were relentless. Most of the men were dragged back into the holes. The rest were cleaned up by those cursed worms that owned that field. Three were trapped on a high point, neither able to advance nor retreat, and there they stayed. How they changed over the years or why they have not yet died, I do not know. But you saw what had become of the one of those men when we escaped."

"The giant?"

"There are two others. Let us hope we do not cross their paths anytime soon. If they have any capacity for thought I am sure that they will not remember us in a positive light."

Kytann stopped and pointed Max forward as the trees rustled up ahead near the crossroads. As they had hoped, something emerged from the dense forest. Max braced as the tree line opened up near the wolves.

His arrow was already aimed at the point of entry when the most unexpected thing happened. Instead of a giant bear emerging from the forest, a large man in a monk's cloak with a halberd came running out of the trees. Although Max was too far away to make out facial expressions it was clear that both the man and the wolves were surprised. In Max's mind Kytann shouted, "Don't shoot!" Max could then hear him giving the wolves orders to surround the large man but not attack, that this was some sort of a trap.

The man was quickly surrounded by the wolves, who circled him weaving in and out of their braided ring. Although the man had the halberd, it hung low to the ground as if it were too heavy for him to wield. It took only a moment for Max to understand that the man was doomed.

He was defenseless and would die. Kytann stayed silent as if waiting for something yet to come. He had seen the carnage at his cave from the last encounter of his wolves with one of the monks. If he lost his wolves to the monk's halberd, what would he use as bait to draw out the bear? Then he smiled and hunched down and bounded out toward the wolves. As he left, Max heard in his mind, "The man will be our bait. Do not shoot him or let him see you. Shoot only the bear."

Max watched as Kytann quickly moved in behind the pack. The circle of wolves began to tighten as one wolf after another came in close enough for the man to reach them with the halberd, but he could not wield it. After several passes the wolves came in closer. With each individual pass the wolves bit or tore at the man's arms and legs. Soon his body dripped with blood from deep cuts, but none of them fatal. Max understood. The man was to be kept alive.

The man took many cuts and began to wobble on his feet. He fell to one knee, using the halberd to hold himself up. It was then that the man began to sing.

Max was so far away he could barely hear his voice, but the song seemed to amplify in his mind, along with visions of the man's life. The man sang of his love of the bear as images of his childhood passed through Max's mind. He sang of a mother who tragically died. The boy in the vision looked strangely familiar. The wolves continued to attack, and then one of them dropped dead at John's feet, a throwing knife run through his head.

Max looked up into the trees above the man and saw a bush of hair perched high in the trees readying to throw another knife. The silhouette was unmistakable. Franz lived! The song continued to play in Max's mind, the vision of a bear comforting the man who had just lost his wife. The bear was beautiful. A tear came to Max's eye as he recognized John in the vision. John was the bloodied man being attacked! Anger flushed through Max's face as the arrow pointed toward one of the circling wolves and he let loose. The arrow caught the wolf in mid stride, and like the giant Max had shot earlier, the wolf turned to ash.

Another smaller monk then emerged from the forest wielding a broad sword. The wolves fell like rain as the sword sung through the carnage. Once the younger monk had finished the wolves, she took down her hood. It was Mary! She stood in front of John to protect him from Kytann, but the great wolf did not move, seemingly mesmerized by John's song that continued on. As the song lingered to an end, painting a beautiful picture of the bear saving John's life, Kytann seemed to wake from his trance. His growl shook the trees as his head bent down toward Mary.

Max turned his next arrow toward Kytann but before he could loose the arrow the great bear emerged from the forest behind the bloody ruin that was John. The bear was larger and more majestic than Max could have imagined. The great bear stood up on his hind legs and roared loud. Nearby trees were torn from their roots from the power of the roar. In Max's mind he heard Kytann's voice commanding him, "Shoot him now." The voice was almost hypnotic, and although Max fought the thought with all his will the arrow slowly moved to target Soman. The great bear looked toward Max and smiled. Max's heart melted at the sight.

"Shoot me in the leg, Max."

Without thinking the arrow flew. The black arrow went deep into the bear's massive hind leg, but he did not even flinch.

Kytann stepped back with both joy and surprise, waiting for the bear to turn to ash. But the bear did not. Soman pointed to the arrow and Mary advanced toward him, and with several heaves pulled it from his leg while keeping her sword trained on the wolf.

It was then that the great bear spoke. "You have lived a lie for so long, Kytann, that you have become the lie. I now sentence you to the truth."

Soman opened his arms and a bright and glorious light emerged from his body illuminating all around him. And then he began to sing. As the song began, all were taken to a dark place before the creation of the world. Hidden from view was the Old One, whose hand reached out and gave a man full of light a scroll. As Max watched he knew the man of light to be the bear, although he could not explain why. It was the most beautiful thing he had ever seen.

The man of light then opened the scroll and it unrolled into the depths of the darkness with no end in sight. The man of light then began to sing, and from his words great stars were formed. The backdrop exploded with light and color as the universe was sung into existence. The melody of the song was sweet and as the massive stars moved about within the vastness of space they seemed to keep pace with the rhythm of the song that gave them birth.

Although Max saw the vision as if he were there, he also watched Kytann as the song went on. The wolf's tic, near his neck began to spasm violently as if the shame from within for denying the glorious beginnings of the universe was tearing him apart from the inside. Soman's face showed no anger toward the wolf as he writhed in pain, only a profound sadness as the truth destroyed the wolf from within.

The song continued with the creation of heaven and the great throne of the man of light. Then in a more intimate way the man of light sat on the throne and with and through the song created beings one by one in the heavenly realm. It was only several creatures into the song that Kytann himself was shown to be created. He only vaguely resembled the wolf he had now become. Then he was a glorious golden creature with bright rainbow eyes that glistened as they reflected the light from the one who created him. The creature sung out a song of glory as soon as his mouth had been formed and the man of light embraced him.

Max now looked toward the wolf that Kytann had become. His painful writhing had now contorted all of his body. The spasms from the shame of his betrayal were so violent that Max could hear the massive bones from within his flesh snap under the strain. Max caught glimpse of one of his red eyes that burned with a fire from within and told of incomprehensible pain. At that moment Max took pity on the creature and deep within himself he wished for mercy on the beast.

Soman turned his head toward Max as if to acknowledge the wish and Kytann burst into flame. The stench of singed hair soon filled the stifled air of the trail. As Soman's song shifted the vision of other things faded and a strong cool breeze raced down the trail stoking the fire. Nearby trees burst into flame from the heat, and the breeze swirled their fire around Kytann. The wolf turned what was left of his neck before he was gone and looked into the eyes of Max with an eye that was no longer red, but filled with the colors of the rainbow. With that the fire overtook him and what was left of the wolf was now only a fine ash that the breeze then swirled into the air toward the sun that now shone brightly above.

Once the ash of the wolf was gone, Soman turned and went to John. "You did well, John." The great bear hugged him, and held him tight. John's wounds began to heal while in the embrace of the great bear.

"Why could I not kill the wolves? The head of the halberd was so heavy I could barely lift it from the ground. Now it is like a light stick." John lifted the weapon up and twirled it as if it had no weight at all.

Soman smiled and walked toward Max, who stood nearby with his bow neither advancing nor retreating. Max looked down in shame for shooting his arrow at someone so beautiful as the great bear. With a lurch so fast Max could barely see him move, Soman leapt forward and scooped up Max with his forepaw and held him high, close to his face.

"Max is precious to me. It was his path to see my beauty through your story, John. You suffered that Max would live."

Soman threw Max high in the air near the tips of the trees. The warmth of the sun caught Max's face for a weightless moment before he fell and was brought securely back into Soman's arms.

Soman brought Max close to his noble face. "Do not be ashamed of shooting the arrow. It was necessary for Kytann to see me pierced with his weapon for him to see the full truth. You are mine, Max, and I shall never let you go."

Tears filled Max's eyes and he embraced Soman and together they wept.

Soman set Max down near John and Mary and Franz, where they embraced and laughed and cried as they each told their story of their time in the forest. Soman then stood high and looked down the wide trail toward the darkness that Kytann had created.

"All of the creation screams out to me of the evil brought into this world through the trees that Kytann planted with my own blood. The earth that has been forced to endure the indignity of these tainted roots for eons yearns for justice. The time has now come to cleanse this world of the fruits of Kytann's shameful acts. The time has now come to destroy the black trees of Kytann." Soman looked back upon the four. "I send you to destroy these trees and cleanse the earth of the evil that they have brought forth."

John, Mary, and Franz lifted their weapons with yells of excitement, anxious to start their next adventure, but Max was quiet. He knew of what guarded the black tree and was terrified of returning.

Soman, knowing Max's mind, bent down close to him. "You have seen the beauty of my face. You are now a path runner. Do not be afraid of the evils you have seen that lie upon your path. You saw my mighty power only moments ago. I will always be with you, Max. You are precious to me. Keep to the path, and keep a strong heart."

Soman then stood tall, pointing back down the wide trail. "The first of the black trees lies that way through the den of Kytann into the depths of the dark forest." With that Soman bid the four farewell and disappeared into the thick of the forest.

CHAPTER 41

After Kytann

The next morning the four found themselves at the edge of the dark plains that marked the former territory of Kytann. It had not yet been even a full day since he had been reduced to ashes and the darkness of the forest was already beginning to recede. Mary looked out onto the plain that she and Aeneas had traveled over only a short time ago. The land was still barren, studded with tree stumps and mud covered logs strewn haphazardly over the dark land. The teeth marks of Kytann could still be seen on the sides of some trees where he had borne down on them and ripped them from the earth. Patches of light now peaked through the canopy up above filling the land with spots of light, light the earth had not seen for hundreds of years. Mary looked far across the plain toward the hill that held Kytann's old cave. A strong beam of light now lit the high point in the otherwise flat plain, as if to invite the foursome to come and see what it had found.

Mary led her companions along the path she and Aeneas had taken, retelling their story as she walked. The land looks so very different than it did when I first saw it just a few days ago, she realized. The overwhelming darkness of the field that had unnerved her so with Aeneas was now only an unkempt wasteland.

They arrived at the stone wall that marked the upward climb to the cave. The blood of the many wolves that had died at the edge of Mary's sword had now dried, with patches of sun baking the once muddy path to a stone hard surface that had a purplish hue from the wolf blood that mortared its surface. Mary arrived at the top of the path first and looked down over the cliff that she had once jumped. Some of the mist had now cleared in the depths of the ravine and she could see the rapids of the river flowing far below. She wondered at how she had survived such a fall. She remembered coming up out of the water and finding the great bear there waiting for her. She filled with warmth at the thought, but that warmth evaporated as she turned and saw Aeneas' staff leaning against the side of the cave entrance. At the foot of the staff lay Aeneas' brown robe and scattered on the robe were the monk's bones, chewed clean by the wolves. The bright light that they had seen from afar now bathed the bones in light, making them almost glow in the backdrop of the dark cave.

Mary knelt down with tears in her eyes and carefully stacked the bones on the old robe. As she picked up one of the bones she noted a speck of green. It was a sapling now growing in the forest's newfound light. The four buried Aeneas' bones in his robe at the entrance of the cave next to the fledgling tree. They marked his grave with his staff buried halfway into the soil and told stories of their friend who was now gone. The four companions were quiet as they made their way through the rest of Kytann's territory and no one said more than a few words until they hit the green of the forest again.

That next morning Max took the lead toward the dark of the forest. He had found the path that he and Kytann had originally taken. Unlike the forest around Kytann's cave which was recovering from the darkness that weighed so heavily on its bows, the old forest within which they now walked seemed to cling tightly to the deepening shades of grey that defined its borders. They could see only a little light trickling through the canopy above.

The group came to a halt as they approached a footprint of a beast that must have been at least as large as Kytann. The print was three feet long and pressed deep within the earth, speaking to the enormous weight of the monster that had created it. The claw marks at the forefront of the print drove deep within the ground, smooth holes puncturing the rocky soil. Max knelt down to the print and reached his arm down one of the puncture marks but could not reach the bottom. He looked back toward his three companions and shook his head.

Mary raised her sword, looking down the trail where the tracks led. The trail darkened in the distance. No signs of life could be seen. "Did you see that thing when you were here last?"

Max shook his head. "Only the worms and the giant." Max was silent for a moment. "But Kytann was always on guard, watching for something. Something that even he feared. He spoke of darker beasts that lived beyond the black tree that came to be from an ancient curse."

Little more was said that day as they walked deeper into the forest. That evening they camped at the edge of the dark plain that led to the black tree. In the distance they could hear the thundering howls of huge beasts far off in the dark. They lit no fire that night, hoping to draw as little attention to themselves as possible. John had carried with him some dried fish that they ate under the dark trees.

Max looked out over the field. "It is a long run to the tree from here." Max reached out toward the open field and scooped up a handful of sifted dirt. "The worms that guard the tree are fierce. They could even have overwhelmed Kytann. I think that is why he had not ventured back to the tree for so many years."

Mary looked out into the darkness. "The howls seem to come from beyond the field. I wonder what sort of beasts could howl so loud?"

John smiled as he sat polishing the blade of his halberd. "I have seen many things on the narrow path. Many times I thought I would die, but I followed the path and I did not." John paused for a moment and the group fell silent. "Soman sent us on this quest. He sustains all things with his song. If we cannot trust in him, then there is nothing that we can trust in. It is that trust that made me alive. I feel it as a warmth within me, yearning for the next adventure. I would rather die than lose it."

Mary looked down at the ground. "Aeneas followed the path and he died."

John looked up from the blade on his halberd, which seemed to shine even in the absence of light. "Aeneas followed the path to its end. All we can do is the same. But I do not think our path will end here." John ran his thumb over the blade of the halberd. Even though it looked razor sharp it would not draw his blood. "My end will come soon enough. For now we must prepare for our next adventure. We will sleep tonight, and set off for the tree at dawn. The tree thrives in darkness. We will attack it in the light."

CHAPTER 42

The Shadow Beast

Dawn came without light. John and Franz had slept soundly, but Max and Mary rested little over the night. Max stood and looked out over the dark plain.

"The tree is out in that direction. I had the light from Kytann's white paw to light the way before. We will need to risk lighting a torch or we will never find it." Max grabbed an old branch the size of his arm and wrapped some cloth around it that was still saturated from the oil from the farm house.

Mary looked down at Max, clearly concerned. "They will see us."

Max looked up. "We will never find the tree without the light. We will have to risk being seen."

Max rose and raised the torch. The light flickered over the faces of the four, casting long shadows behind them. The air seemed heavier, as if the forest itself held its breath for what was to come. Without saying a word Max began to jog out onto the field. John scooped up Franz with one hand loading him onto one shoulder and followed close behind. Mary carried the rear with her sword over her shoulder, looking behind every fourth step.

One hundred yards into the dark plain Franz caught the wisp of a shadow from the corner of his eye. He turned but there was nothing. Pulling back his hair with one of his knives, he looked out into the dark and after several moments he slowly pointed his free hand to the right.

Mary followed his arm with her eyes. At first she saw nothing but a wall of black, and then the wall of black moved. Mary stopped in her tracks for a moment as she tried to take in how big what she was looking at must be. Its shadowy form defied a defined shape in the dark, but its presence towered into the sky as high as the farmhouse. Mary turned toward Max and yelled, "Run!"

Max needed no explanation to hasten his pace. The three sprinted into the dark toward a massive pillar far off in the distance. The dark tree was still a long way off.

Mary turned again and the wall of black was now almost upon them. In the dim light of the torch she saw the gleam of fangs that hung from a foul mouth a full body's length. She could now smell the fetid smell of the beast's breath, a heated fume of rotting flesh. Remembering John's words, she stopped her run and turned toward the giant beast, raising her sword.

The shadow beast stopped for a moment and roared. If the beast had second thoughts, it must have let them go quickly as it rushed toward Mary with intensified fury. A giant claw swept down from the heavens above. Mary jumped and rolled as the claw dug deep within the earth. Again the beast unleashed a deafening roar. It was not used to missing its prey.

From above Mary could see the other claw coming down toward her. She braced her legs firmly in the soil beneath her and raised the sword. She saw the metal of the blade almost glow in front of her eyes as if the sword yearned to cut deep within the beast. A claw the size of Mary came down hard and swift. The sword pulled Mary to the side and fell with a speed so furious Mary's eyes could barely follow its path. The sword sliced through the arm of the beast, cutting the claw clean off.

The beast rose up on its hind legs and howled into the dark heavens above. The claw, now free of its master, bounded far down the plain, like a boulder bouncing down a hill.

Mary held her ground, holding her sword high as if to taunt the giant beast in closer. The shadowy beast was only too happy to oblige and fell from its lofty heights toward Mary. The beast landed only yards away. The ground shook as its single paw sunk deep within the earth. Mary could feel the hot air from its rotten breath right over her. She moved the sword directly above her and then the beast let out another deafening howl.

Ash sprinkled down on Mary like snow as she looked up and saw the beast's shoulder disintegrating above her. She looked back to see Max reloading an arrow. That was all the invitation she needed as she ran headlong into the beast with her sword raised. The sword fell with glee across the hind foot of the beast cutting through tendon and bone. The beast now toppled left and right trying to maintain balance on its one hind leg.

A blur of hair passed underneath Mary as Franz ran straight toward the beast's leg and leapt halfway up the beast. Using his knives as climbing tools he moved higher and higher up the beast, clearly making toward its head.

The beast howled again. Another of Max's arrows had found a home in the beast's chest. Again ash fell from the sky. Mary turned toward the weakened leg and found that John had already made it there. His halberd fell, and like the sword, it cut through the flesh of the beast as if it was moving through air. The hind leg fell free to the ground and the beast now began a slow tilt, like a great tree after a final ax blow slowly making its way to the earth.

As the beast fell it swung with its only remaining claw toward Mary. It had caught Mary by surprise and she was not able to turn in time to parry. The claw then suddenly diverted its path toward the beast's face, missing Mary by only inches. She looked up toward the face of the beast now falling toward her, and there riding on its brow was Franz gouging out one of its dark, soulless eyes with two of his knives.

The beast wailed in misery, now spinning in its fall. John ran toward Mary and held up his halberd which sunk deep within the head of the beast as it hit the ground. A cloud of dust filled the air, now silent, as the beast lay motionless in the soft soil of the plain. From the cloud of dust bounded out a small creature carrying two bloodied knives who smiled and took his place back on John's shoulder.

The four looked at each other and then at the beast that lay on the path behind them. They broke into laughter but stopped quickly when they heard the furious howls of the creatures of the dark, which now filled the air with such a loud sound it could almost be felt. The four turned toward the towering pillar in the distance and ran. For a moment the howling quieted, but then they could feel the very earth beneath their feet shake. Mary looked back to see a whole legion of shadowy beasts advancing toward them with reckless abandon. She turned her head and focused on the tree and ran.

They made only several hundred yards before the advancing horde of monsters was nearly upon them. Mary's heart had been given hope when they felled the shadow beast, but how could they defend themselves from such a wild horde? John reached the tree first and raised the halberd, which fell fast as it sliced through the massive girth of the tree.

The beasts in the distance howled as if only now understanding the purpose of their trespassers. They picked up their pace.

John's halberd fell again and a massive wedge of black wood fell to the ground. Each of John's blows swung deep within the tree. "This tree is so wide I will need more time to bring it to the ground," he told the three children.

Max looked out into the advancing wall of death and drew an arrow and loosed it toward the advancing horde. The howl of the arrow's target soon followed as the beast's front leg turned to ash. The beast tripped and was soon overrun by the stampede of evil that was now running all out.

John again let the halberd fall and again a giant wedge of wood fell to the ground. John was keeping a good pace, but he would not get through the trunk before the horde of beasts overran them.

Mary looked at the oncoming beasts and a piece of her wanted to charge out into the frenzy, but then she looked back toward John chopping away at the tree as if he were totally oblivious to the oncoming doom. Without a further thought she ran toward John and sliced her sword down into the huge girth of the tree. Another wedge of wood fell to the ground. They sliced down again and deep within the tree the groan of over a thousand years of cursed growth emerged.

"It's weakening," John said. Mary nodded.

They had cut through half the tree. John remembered what Max had said about the tree's bark burning like acid. He jumped over the skin of the tree and landed on both feet onto the wide surface he had just cut. He waited for a moment, half expecting to melt away, but nothing happened. He motioned Mary to follow as they cut deeper into the tree's giant core.

The beasts were now only fifty yards away. Max unleashed arrow after arrow as beasts fell in the charging line and were then trampled by the horde that was now almost upon them. Franz, who had been quiet after his part in felling the shadow beast, took off and ran headlong toward the charging beasts. Halfway between the tree and the advancing monsters he stopped and yelled with all his might, both arms outstretched with knives in hand.

* * * * *

It was then that the earth began to shake. John and Mary did not notice as they chopped away at the tree, but Max took notice. He had felt that tremor before. He called to Franz to return to the tree, but the sound of the advancing beasts made any shouts useless. Max looked down at the loose dirt rattling about his feet. He then looked out toward Franz. *The worms are coming.*

Max pulled another arrow out. As he did he noticed for the first time that there were as many arrows in the quiver as when he had started. He was grateful, but it would not matter. He let loose arrow after arrow, focusing now on the center of the onslaught, trying to carve a wedge into the attack line in an attempt to save Franz. The beasts were only several yards away from Franz now, and Franz held his ground, yelling into the deafening silence of the moment.

Max looked out at Franz. *It will be over soon.* He pulled out one more arrow as the very earth erupted from below. Only moments before the beasts would have overrun Franz, the giant worms erupted from the earth, sending the beasts flailing like grease sputtering from a hot pan. A great cloud of dust overtook Franz. Max could see nothing but the angry beasts being thrown left and right in the air by the fangs of the giant worms. Max's heart sank as he saw the advancing cloud and then his heart jumped as he made out Franz now riding on the back of one of the worms, slashing into the beast as he made his way through the dusty field.

The worms seemed to understand Franz and now were mounting an organized attack on the beasts. *How is this possible?* Max was certain that if the beasts had not killed him the worms most certainly would have, but now the worms fought with them? The worms fought with such fury it was as if the very earth were angry at the evil that now lay upon it. It was then that Max understood that the worms were not mindless beasts bent on evil and destruction but an extension of Soman's creation that had been defiled by the tree and now the foul beasts. The worms wanted what they wanted. To be rid of the tree.

A great cracking sound echoed from behind. Max looked back to see John and Mary jumping from the tree as it began to slowly fall toward the frenzy of worm and beast. From far above the creaking of branches overtook the sound of the battle. A sliver of light cracked open above as the canopy of the black tree was broken. The sliver of light quickly became a rapid sunrise as the light of the sun shown down upon the plain for the first time in over a thousand years. The light reached the beasts, some of which burst into flame. They howled as if tortured by a thousand knives as they wildly ran for the darkness of the caves beyond the great tree.

As the tree hit the ground it shook the earth, raising John and his companions several feet high from the impact. Mary looked out onto the field, which was bathed in soft light. The beasts were gone. As the sun fell upon the remaining worms they shrank back to the size of earthworms that were only slightly larger than normal. There in the middle of the field covered in worms was Franz with his two hands held up high in victory.

John looked out at Franz and laughed at the sight.

Max walked back to John. "Did you ever have any doubt?"

John slapped Max on the back as he continued to laugh. "Doubt? I had no time to doubt. I was chopping down a tree."

CHAPTER 43

Ariel

Max smiled and looked down upon the stump of the black tree that was covered in sunlight. The sun burned into the exposed wood, leaving a smoking trail as the light carved into the surface of the stump. As Max looked on he realized he was looking upon a map being drawn from the light above. The rest of the company looked down upon the stump as the light carved away an elaborate map which started at the site of the fallen tree and led to a distant land where another giant tree stood tall, deep within a range of mountains. Between them and the next tree lay thousands of miles of terrain, much of which crossed over mountains of unimaginable height and great winding rivers that wound through deep ravines. John took his halberd and pointed toward the destination of their next adventure. As he did a knife sunk deep within the tree on the map. John turned with a smile at Franz, who stood with his hands on his hips as if to ask, "What are we waiting for?"

Mary sighed. "It will take years to cross over to Kytann's second tree." Mary ran her sword over the map on the stump. "How are we to make it through these mountains? The map does not give us a path to take. We could be lost in those mountains for years looking for a pass. Aren't maps supposed to give us a path to follow?"

Max looked down at the map, searching for a line of some sort over the intricate terrain that the light had carved on the black wood. He ran his hand over the map thinking that he might be able to feel what they could not see and carefully tracked what he imagined would be the route they would take. The quality of the map was without equal. As he ran his fingers over the lowlands and the rest of the mountains, he could almost feel the trees beneath his fingertips. The snow covered peaks felt cold as his fingers ran over their jagged teeth. As his hand finally met Kytann's second tree a sense of calm and melancholy rushed over him. He pulled his finger off the tree looking around at the others to see if they saw what he had just felt, but they were busy discussing what they would need to forge a path through the mountains.

Max drew his eyes back to the stump on the map. As a cloud passed overhead the light on the wood dimmed and Max could make out a fine line in the grain of the wood that led to what looked like a worm hole, in the opposite direction from where they had been looking. At first he mistook the route for a variation of the natural grain of the wood but there were no other lines that followed along it. And the more he stared at it, the more it seemed to have a faint glimmer as if it were lined with silver.

But it doesn't make any sense that the silver line could be the path— does it? Max asked himself. It was heading the opposite direction from where they wanted to go and dead ended in a hole. Max's eyes then grew wide and he raced over to the end of the map toward the next dark tree. As he looked closely he could now make out the same fine silver line weaving out from the tree into a nearby mountain range and then, like the first line, disappearing into a small hole. Max put his finger on the hole and could feel a breeze pushing against his finger. Max pulled his finger away and looked up to John and Mary. "I have found the path."

John and Mary stopped mid-sentence and looked toward Max. Mary looked down at the map near where Max was kneeling with a skeptical eye. "Where?" was all that she asked.

Max drew a line with his finger along the silver line from the black tree to the nearby hole in the mountain.

"How is that little line going to get us across all of this?" Mary's furrowed eyebrows told a story of impatient frustration.

Max crawled over to the beginning of the map to the stump on which they stood and followed with his finger the silver line from the stump to a nearby hole that sat in what looked like the foot of a cliff.

Mary was about to say something when John blurted out, "It's a tunnel. The path is a tunnel."

Max smiled and nodded.

Now John's eyebrows furrowed as he looked at the hole near the stump. "Where is that hole from here?"

As Max studied the map he soon realized the source of John's concern. Looking out across the plain and back down at the map and then back out over the plain, Max raised his arm and pointed toward the cliffs at the far edge of it. They were the same cliffs that housed the caves that the monster horde had just run back into.

Mary looked at Max as if to ask, are you crazy? What she did ask was, "You want us to go over there?" Mary pointed toward the caves which now stood in the shadow of the cliff. "In case you didn't notice, that is where all of those … things … just ran into. They are still there, Max."

Max looked up to Mary and said nothing as he tapped his finger on the hole in the wood.

Franz had come near the map and was looking at the hole that Max had found. He took a piece of his robe and started rubbing the silver line. As he cleaned off the soot from where the light had burned the map into the wood, the line could now be clearly seen. The cloud above passed over and as the full light of the sun now hit the map, the silver light shined strong and bright. They each silently agreed, yes, that is the path.

John stood up and looked over to the caves in the shadow of the cliff. "We still have half of the day's light left. Maybe the beasts are deep within the caves licking their wounds." John pointed back down at the hole in the map. "It looks like that thing is right at the entrance of the caves. We don't have to follow the beasts into the caves. We just have to get to the hole."

Franz jumped up on John's shoulder and pulled out one of his knives, pointing it out toward the caves. Mary and Max looked to Franz, who seemed to have no fear, and they felt his sense of adventure flowing into them. John picked up his halberd and began walking across the plain toward the caves that stood about a mile away. Without looking back he waved for the twins to follow and soon they were right by his side.

The walk across the loose dirt of the plain was easy on the feet and they made good time. The caves that they initially saw from afar were much larger than they had imagined, some standing over six times the height of John's old house. The foursome stopped several hundred yards out at the edge of the shadow of the cliff and looked out at the wall of rock that loomed high in the sky. The cliff was more curved than they had thought from afar, forming a semicircle, almost like an amphitheatre around a depression in the ground. Whether that was the hole or not they could not yet know as it was hidden behind a small mound of earth, obstructing their view.

As they walked into the shadow of the cliff they moved more slowly, wary of what might lie in this dark land hidden from the sun. The air grew heavy with the stench of rotten flesh. On the ground they could see the deep tracks of the many beasts that had retreated into the caves only hours ago. Splotches of dark blood laid across the plain, testimony to the destruction caused by the worms in the great battle. They slowly climbed up the mound that had hidden full view of the caves only moments ago. As they crested the mound they saw the glowing yellow and red eyes of the cursed beasts looking out at them from the deep shadows of the caves. In front of the caves was a massive hole thirty feet across. Its walls were as smooth as glass and reflected no light, making the hole seem as if it was made of darkness itself. Circling the hole was a single beast that looked like a cross between a lizard and a lion. It was twice the height of John and was covered with scales of every color that seemed to ripple across its body as it breathed. As the four looked down upon the strange beast, it stopped in its tracks and turned its head toward them. Its scale ruffled like feathers and turned bright red and orange.

Without warning the beast leapt across the giant hole and with only three bounds stood tall only feet away looking down on the sojourners. "Who among you is the wild thing that rides the worms?" The beast lowered his head and turned his golden eye on John, clearly guessing he was the one.

John stepped back and raised his halberd ready to strike. "Do you speak for the monsters that dwell in the caves?"

The beast fluffed his scales, turning them from fire red and orange to a bright gold that matched its golden eyes. "I am not one of the cursed beasts that dwell in the caves. I am Ariel, he who guards the passageway." Ariel again bent down and examined the blade on John's halberd. "I can see from your weaponry that you are in the service of the great bear. I, too, am in the service of the great bear."

Ariel took his front paw and ran it across the cutting edge of the ax head of the halberd. "Your weapons are of no use against me. They are as dull as the ground you walk on. They only cut through that which is evil, and I am most certainly not evil."

John slowly lowered his halberd to the ground. "You know of Soman?"

Ariel looked upon John as if he were joking. "Soman sings all things into existence. All beings who have a mind to think know Soman, whether they know that they do or not. I served Him before the earth was made, before His glorious coming as a man, and before he came in the form of the great bear that you know him as in the present age. But you have not answered my question. Who is the great warrior who rode the worms?" Ariel looked down at Max and Mary studying their faces.

Max blushed as Ariel stared at him and pointed up to Franz in answer to his question. Ariel jumped back in astonishment, drawing his attention to Franz. "The child with the wild hair is the one that leaves the cursed beasts cowering in their caves?" Ariel laughed. "This is truly worthy of a great song. What is your name, little one?"

Franz looked embarrassed at the attention that now focused on him and hid his face in his hair. John smiled, looking up to him as he sat on his shoulder. "The great warrior's name is Franz." John then went on to tell their tale of the last several weeks to Ariel.

Ariel listened carefully as John told their story. "We have known that there would come a time when Soman would destroy the black trees. It is a glorious thing that he has let you be the vehicle of his will. The next tree that you seek is at the other end of the passageway before us."

Ariel walked down to the massive hole that looked like a bottomless glass well. As they hovered over its edge they could only see about three feet in as the darkness of the hole blended in with the black glass that formed its borders. "You must go now while the sun still shines on the plain. The fear that the cursed beasts have of Franz will not be enough to keep them at bay once the light of the sun has passed. They are wild and without remorse. You will surely die if you do not leave now."

* * * * *

John thought of the first time he had walked the narrow path in the forest and had nearly been crushed by the forest closing in behind him. The narrow path stopped for no one. Even now on the edge of the barren plain he felt the rhythm of the path moving him along. Even though they had left the trees they were still very much on the path. And as he had learned in the forest, to stop on the narrow path meant death. Without thinking John began to sing the song Soman had taught him when he first learned to open the path. The beauty of Soman filled him as he set Franz to his side and stepped into the darkness.

It was only half a moment before John was enveloped within the silent emptiness of the void. He continued to sing but could hear nothing, not even the sound of his own voice. He waved his hand over his face and saw nothing. A slow panic began to overcome him as he rubbed his hand on his face but he could feel nothing. He was alone in the void. The emptiness of the darkness was overwhelming, and his heart raced as he contemplated being utterly alone. It was the most frightening experience that John had ever experienced, and more than ever he longed for the comfort of the great bear.

Mary and Max reached out to grab John as he fell but they had not anticipated him leaving so quickly. They looked toward Ariel as if to ask him what to do.

"The warrior will go last." Ariel looked down upon Franz and smiled.

Mary and Max looked at each other and nodded. Without another word they both jumped into to the dark void.

Ariel then leaned down low so that he would be at the level of Franz's ear and whispered something ever so quietly. Franz smiled and rubbed the side of Ariel's face. He then ran back to the mound, turned and drew two knives out as he had held them when he had ridden the worms to victory. He sprinted toward the hole and ten feet before its lip he leapt high in the air and let out a fierce battle cry with his arms outstretched holding his knives.

* * * * *

Ariel watched as the glowing eyes in the caves fled to the deeper places of the earth. As Franz disappeared into the darkness of the hole, Ariel laughed at the sight. This would make for a good song, indeed.

CHAPTER 44

Strange Words

Franz fell freely into the darkness of the hole. He waved his hand in front of his face but could see nothing. The darkness was so complete that even sound seemed to be absorbed into the void. As he fell, it first grew colder, but over time the air seemed to slowly warm. He held his blade out in front of him and could now see a faint glow reflecting from the metal. He looked around him and noticed that the walls of the hole also had within them a faint orange glow. As he fell deeper it seemed that he was speeding up. His hair now whipped above his head from the breeze of his own freefall.

What started as the faintest hint of warmth in the air progressed to a sweltering heat. The sides of the hole now glowed bright yellow as if fire itself had found liquid form and was circling the hole. With the yellow light Franz could now see far down the tube within which he was falling. Far below he could see Mary and Max as dark specks circling within the tube, with a faint speck in the far off distance that he guessed must be John.

Franz then rotated so that he was now falling head first and clasped his hands together out in front of him, making himself as streamlined as he could be. He watched as the specks that he knew to be Max and Mary slowly became larger. As he picked up speed his body seemed to pick up a slow rotation, which he only realized as he watched Mary and Max slowly spinning. It was impossible to know if he was even moving from just looking at the walls of the tube, as one piece looked the same as the next.

Franz had picked up so much speed that when he passed Mary and Max he was only seen as a blur of hair blowing in the wind as he rushed by. In less than a minute he torpedoed past John. The light from the tube now began to lessen, turning from white to yellow and then back to the dull orange where it had started. The air was also changing. There was now a cool and crispness in the wind that Franz cut through, leaving the promise of snow in his nose as he took a deep breath.

Although it was hard to tell, it seemed that he was now slowing down. The walls of the hole had returned to pitch black. Franz looked up and could see the faint glow of stars at the end of the tunnel. Almost as soon as he noticed this he found himself being thrown from the hole high into the night sky. As he reached the apex of his flight he noticed how sharp the stars appeared. They seemed much clearer than he had remembered. Franz then fell to the ground into a pile of snow, causing a puff of steam as his hot robe found some relief in the blue powder that he now found himself in.

As Franz looked around he saw that he was on the side of a snow covered mountain. Jagged peaks stretched out into the night in all directions. It was then that he noticed a hand the size of his own reaching out to help pull him from the snow. Franz let himself be pulled up above the snow and now looked upon a child his size with a shaven head and clothed in a loose maroon robe. The small hand of the child reached over to spread Franz's hair to expose his face. Franz smiled and found a smiling face glowing in the starlight back at him. It was then that John shot out of the hole and landed softly in the snow near the edge of the hole. Max and Mary soon followed.

The small child looked upon those who had come from the great hole and smiled. She then looked back toward Franz. "I am Dorje. You are in my country, called Tibet. We live in a land of very high mountains and thin, cold air. I am the one who has prayed for the delivery of my father from the hidden valley. Your coming was revealed to me in a dream. I also saw a great bear with you in my dream. Is he here with you now?"

Franz looked to the others, not knowing what to say. It was odd to him that he understood the child. He knew her words were foreign and yet he heard them as if they were in his own tongue.

John walked over to the child and knelt down low so that he could see her face. "The great bear has sent us to this foreign land to destroy the black tree."

Dorje looked disappointed. "So the warrior bear has not traveled with you?"

John smiled and took the child's hand in his own. "The great bear travels within our hearts. He is within us and we are with him. What is it that you seek from the great bear?"

"War has broken out in our land. My people have fled to the sacred places in the mountains to find sanctuary. We have wandered in the shadow of the great mountain that touches the sky for years now." Dorje sat down in a clear spot and looked down into the snow, running her finger through the cold powder as she spoke. "Many would have dreams leading them out into the night alone in search of a paradise that promised enlightenment, a freedom from the pain of this world. None have returned. My father was the head of our order. He was the last to leave. Our numbers now dwindle." Dorje looked up at John. "You have been sent by Manjushri to save my people … and to find my father."

Dorje then arose and began walking along a narrow snow covered path alongside the mountain. "You will follow me."

The night was dark. John followed in the rear with his halberd at the ready. They had little choice but to follow the child. Walking the narrow path in the snow, John realized he had a sense of being with Soman. Without thinking he began to sing his song to open the path as he walked.

Dorje stopped and looked back at John. "That is the music I had heard in my dreams." She then turned back toward the path and kept walking, picking up the pace, as if sensing that they were being followed.

It was an hour's walk to her camp on the mountainside in a deep cave. Dorje sat down in front of a fire near the cave's mouth. In the back of the cave the four companions could see a dim light emanating from a smaller fire. Next to that fire sat an old man warming his hands over the flames.

The fire was a welcome sight to Mary. She sat down next to Dorje and invited the child to tell her story of how they ended up in a cave alone in the mountain.

"There was a civil war in our land that left many orphans," Dorje began. Out of love for the children the elders of their families had brought them into the mountains in search of a mystical fertile land that would be hidden from the warlords. She and her father had split off from the group a month ago, and he had set off alone in search of the fertile valley two days ago. "I am out of food," Dorje admitted. She talked of going out into the mountain alone to search for her father and the paradise that had lured them into the mountain so long ago.

Mary began to tell the Dorje of their story, beginning with their time spent with Father Aeneas. She talked of the many hours Aeneas had spent with her telling her the story of the Man in the stained glass windows of the church. She told of the beauty of His life and how His beauty allowed her to find the narrow path. Dorje was in awe as Mary continued to tell their story.

* * * * *

John smiled and looked back at the old man alone in the back of the cave. Dorje seemed content to leave him be. John began to walk back to hear the old man's story, hoping to get a clue as to which direction to continue in search of the black tree. As he came closer he began to understand why the old man was alone. His hunched over body was covered in tattered rags stained with the seeping of sores that covered his back. His hair grew thinly out of his head in patches that did little to cover the dirt of the mountain that stained deeply into his skin. His joints were contorted and swollen. Just to look at him was painful. As John stood next to the man he could hear him babbling. The man's face hung low looking into the fire, drool dripping onto a hot rock below. John knelt down, feeling pity for the man, trying to listen to what he was saying.

The old man's voice was quiet, muffled by a rasp that suggested the health of the inner body matched that of the outer shell. "Sunlight gone … mountains cold … chicken bones and silvery stones … beauty lost, desire gone … fire cold like snow … all is gone, love is gone … chicken bones and silvery stones …"

John sat listening to the man babble for nearly an hour more out of respect and pity for the man than any hope of getting any useful direction from him. The man was clearly mad. It was a wonder that he was even alive in the rugged mountains. John looked back toward the mouth of the cave at where the children sat. It was time to leave the man in his own little world and rejoin the group. As he rose the old man raised his glassy blue eyes up toward John, and John realized the man could not see him. In spite of that, he seems to see right through him.

"What is it that you seek in the mountain?"

John jerked back for a moment, surprised that the old man even knew he was there. John knelt back down close to the old man, his hope of finding a path to the tree rekindled. "We seek a great black tree that grows nearby." John looked closely into the man's sightless eyes, wondering what he saw through eyes that no longer let in the light of day.

"No one desires the black trees … black trees and itchy fleas … chicken bones and silvery stones … beauty rusts … cold stones and broken bones … desire fades … chicken bones and silvery stones … a great bear's love all alone." The old man reached for a stick and started stirring the embers.

John was slowly getting up as the man was babbling but he stopped at the mention of the great bear. Was it possible that Soman had been here?

The old man bent his head back down. "Desire lingers on the edges of beauty. Where do you find beauty?"

It was odd to John to see the lips of the man speaking one language and hearing it in his own language in his head. He knew it was the work of Soman that allowed this, but there was still an eerie feeling to it. And why was the man trying to play word games with him? He would play along and perhaps the old man would eventually give him what he needed.

He did not have to think long to answer the old man. Long days running the narrow path had taught him clearly where he found beauty, though he doubted the man would understand his answer. "In the face of Soman."

The old man continued to stir the coals, seemingly looking into the fire with his sightless eyes. "From beauty comes desire, from desire comes love, none can be had without the other. Why do you seek direction instead of following beauty? Seek your beauty in the face of the wind and your path will lead you where you need to go … go row lickety bow … chicken bones and silvery stones." And with that the old man grew silent and would say no more.

With that John walked back to the children around the larger fire and sat down. He looked out at the mouth of the cave. A light snow had begun to fall. As the light of the newborn day began to shine through the snow he could hear the wind picking up outside.

"We will need to leave as soon as it is light outside. The map on the black tree showed that the next tree we seek must be close by. It would be better to find it in the light of day." John rubbed his arms to warm them by the fire.

Dorje looked up at John. "I will follow you on your quest. I have nothing here and I have already told you I am out of food."

John looked down at Dorje with concern. "Where we are going there will be danger." Dorje looked back up at him with the shallow cheeks of one who had not eaten well for months. She would starve if they left her. John nodded, but then looked toward the back of the cave. It was dark. The old man's fire must have gone out. "What will come of the old man if we leave him alone?"

Dorje gave John a queer smile. "What old man?"

"The one deep within the cave." John pointed back to where the fire had been.

Dorje stood and waved her hand over herself. "I am all that is left. There is no one else."

John was silent for a moment. Had he imagined the whole thing? Dorje looked at him and he could tell she realized that he had seen something in the back of the cave. Dorje held up her hand. "Walk with me to the back of the cave and we will see what there is to see."

The two walked to the back of the cave not saying a word to one another. There at the back of the cave they found the embers of the small fire still warm, but the old man was not to be found. In his place lying against that wall of the cave was a small curved sword that had two curves like a figure S and a metal flame at its tip. Dorje stepped back as if she recognized the sword and was afraid.

John bent down to pick up the sword and looked it over. It was light, like the rest of their weapons. He rubbed his fingers over the hilt. It was made of the same cool black wood that made up the staff of his halberd. On the side of the blade was the same writing that was on his halberd's ax blade. On the hilt was a single inscription. John could not read it but in his mind he heard the name "Dorje." John raised his eyebrow as he looked over at the young child. With her name on the sword it would seem that she had a role to play in their adventure.

John handed over the sword. "It has your name on it. It belongs to you."

Dorje backed away. "It is a magical blade. I saw it in the war. I do not want it."

"We all walk a path in this life that we do not control. I do not know why this sword was left for you. But I do know that you must take it." John knelt down and pulled Dorje close to him as he pointed toward the mouth of the cave. "I do not know what awaits us out there, but I promise you that we will face it together."

Dorje smiled and hugged John. She tentatively took the sword and ran one finger along the blade. "It is dull. It does not even cut my finger."

John smiled and led Dorje back to the group. "That is because it was not designed to cut your finger."

When they returned to the fire Franz ran to see Dorje's new sword. Max and Mary were already at the edge of the cave looking into the blowing snow. It was blowing so hard that all they could see was a white wall of light at the mouth of the cave.

John pulled his hood over his head and went to join Max and Mary.

Max looked depressed. "We will never find anything in this weather. We are likely to get lost and freeze to death."

Mary nodded. "The wind is so strong we would not even be able to stand in it without being blown over."

John's eyes widened. What had the old man said of the wind? "Seek your beauty in the face of the wind." John then walked up to the edge of the snow, faced into the wind and began to think of the beauty of Soman. The others gathered in close. John then took a step into the blowing snow as it parted, just as the trees did in the forest. They had found the narrow path in the mountain.

CHAPTER 45

The White Swarm

John began a slow jog with everyone keeping close to him on the path. He could not see where they were going and for a moment imagined himself walking off the side of a cliff. He slowed for a moment but then hastened the pace. The path had never led him into something that he could not handle. Without the wind blowing on them they soon warmed as they ran.

The path led them up high into the mountain over boulders and through what John thought were narrow crevices, although the blowing snow kept him from knowing exactly what they were passing. The sun shone brightly on the snow as it whipped around them, but as in the forest the sky was clear directly above. John found himself hoping for the path to open up to a small green oasis with blackberry bushes, but they had been three hours on the path now without a break.

John could now feel a slight down slope on the path. As he looked back his foot punched through a thin layer of snow and the path floor suddenly opened up beneath them. Once John had broken through the shell of ice the entire floor of the path gave way, releasing them to the openness that lay below. They tumbled through the cool still air landing on a smooth sloped chute of ice that had once drained the upper mountain before the ice ceiling that they had fallen through had been formed. All of the party was now spinning and rolling trying to relocate forward. John took several kicks to the head as the entire group torpedoed down the steep ice chute. As the mountain curved they slid from side to side, and John now had no idea which direction they were going. Far ahead he could see a bright light as the chute merged with the sky. As they drew closer, the ice walls around them glowed a faint blue, promising sky ahead.

Moments before they reached the edge of light John could now see that the hole of light emptied out the side of a cliff. They were now moving so fast there was no time to do anything but look straight ahead as they popped out of the side of a crevice in the mountain into the open sky. The snow was not falling within the crevice of the mountain. Thousands of feet below they could see the tips of snow covered trees winding along what must be a river bed in the summer time. The opposite wall of the crevice approached fast, a solid wall of grey rock. John prepared himself for the impact, picturing their bodies being violently thrown against the stone like so many eggs smashed against a wall. As they descended slightly they passed by a large rock jutting out from the cliff that had cast a shadow on the face of the cliff hiding the opening into the side of the mountain. John and the entire party jetted into this cave where the ice chute continued. It hurled them left and right for over a mile until it finally leveled off onto a giant underground frozen lake. The group now sat in the dark on a smooth plane of ice that stretched out as far as the darkness would allow them to see.

Franz was the first to arise on the dark ice. He stood in a wide stance, gauging the slickness of his foothold. Both arms were spread wide with knives in hand ready for whatever atrocity awaited them in the dark. Over a foot beneath him he could see the cold white glow of tiny fluorescent fish swimming in a school. As they passed out of sight another school took their place as if they were being swept along a river under the ice.

John rolled onto his belly trying to gain purchase on the slippery ice with both hand and foot. Having no success, he took his halberd and spiked the spear portion into the ice. He used it as a pole and climbed up. The spear of the halberd sunk deep into the ice. Both he and Franz saw it pierce the darkness of the lake and they tensed. Ariel had told them at the hole that their blades could only pierce that which was evil. Deep cracks began to spread away from where the halberd had pierced the ice like a growing spider web. A great creaking noise could be heard from below as the ice began to shift.

Franz saw another school of fish swim by in the same line, looked at Mary and Max, and then pointed in the direction of the fish with his knife. Mary and Max could now feel the sway of the great sheet of ice loosening its foundation from its mountain prison. They needed no further prompting.

"Dorje, hold onto John's legs!" whispered Max. John had turned over on his back and Max and Mary threw Dorje on John's legs as if he were a giant sled. John pulled out his halberd and the ice shook. A geyser of water shot through the ice where the halberd had just been pulled. Max and Mary pushed John down the ice. Franz leapt high in the air and landed on his feet just in front of John, sliding forward as if he were riding a wave.

Dorje held her sword out into the dark. The golden flame on the tip of the curved blade burst into a living flame of white, lighting the enormous cavern they now found themselves in. She was blinded at first from the brightness of the flame. As her eyes adjusted she whispered, "I wish I had not illuminated what lies ahead."

They all gazed upon great stalactites of ice hanging high above them from the cavern roof. They were speckled with white as if adorned by many diamonds. As if on cue, the spots of white erupted from the stalactites of ice like snow being blown from a field by a strong wind. The white spots then took wing and cried out into the cavern. Bloodcurdling screeches echoed over the lake. The white creatures swarmed high overhead building numbers and speed as others joined from their perches on the icy spears of the cavern's dome.

As he was looking up, John took his halberd and began to use it as a paddle on the smooth ice, propelling them faster and faster across the surface of the lake. The swarm of flying creatures now moved as a single mass high above, building momentum for their dark purpose. Like a hammer hitting an anvil they struck the base of an ice stalactite in line with their path. The great mass of ice twenty feet in diameter and at least a hundred feet in length shivered at the mighty blow. Puffs of ice then erupted at its base as it broke and began to fall. Many of the flying creatures that had been at the hitting edge of the swarm fell lifeless on the ice around them. Their bodies had neither feather nor hair and their skin was a slick smooth white. Their feet and the edges of their wings, which spread ten feet across, sported long talons that spiked into the ice on impact. Their eyes were small and black, and each had a snout instead of a beak. Fangs as long as a man's hand hung from their limp jaws as they lay dead on the ice.

John dug the halberd deep in the ice like an oar, steering himself and the rest hard to the right. The massive spear of ice fell as if in slow motion in front and to the left of the group as they sped along the surface of the ice. As it impacted with the lake the ice buckled and large sheets of ice tilted high in every direction, creating chaos over the dark waters of the lake. The once flat lake now leaned in toward the ice pillar that had awoken it from its dark slumber.

John and his companions veered to the left toward the ice spear, picking up speed as they slid down the smooth icy surface. Behind the pillar of ice John could see an opening at the edge of the cavern at the end of the underground river that Franz found earlier. It was their only chance for escape.

They continued to pick up speed as they slid down and around the sloped ice and skirted the pillar like a stream of water racing around a bowl trying to miss the drain. High above, the swarm of white creatures circled the massive cavern and headed toward an ice stalactite that hung over the cavern's outlet.

* * * * *

Max saw the swarm's target and understood its motive. The creatures were trying to trap them in the cavern. He held on to John with his legs as he drew a black arrow and with careful aim let it fly into the midst of the swarm. The arrow hissed as it cut through beast after beast in its path. The creatures screeched an angry cry as the swarm broke apart scattering across the dome of the cavern. The pale monsters that had been pierced fell burning onto the surface of the lake. The flame that engulfed them was so hot that they melted through its smooth surface, creating small pools of open water where they fell.

Max's hair whipped in the wind as they quickly approached the hole in the cavern, their hope for escape. High above, the swarm was now reforming, but this time the stalactites above were not their target. Like an angry beast wounded in battle, the swarm of white creatures dove down toward the group as they neared the exit. Mary turned as she continued to slide along with the group and held out her sword, ready to defend their party.

To the group's surprise Dorje climbed over John and stood at her side with her sword held high, just as Mary held her sword. Dorje looked up to Mary and smiled. Mary smiled back. "If this is to be our last stand, we'll make it a glorious stand together," Mary whispered to her.

Thirty yards ahead lay a small opening in the side of the cavern. The ice was still tilted toward their target as they slid closer and closer to freedom. The first of the white creatures to reach them felt the bite of Mary's blade as the steel separated head from neck. As before, the sword knew its job and directed Mary's blows with precision. Max reloaded and shot arrow after arrow into the hoard. The arrows hissed in the air like a white hot piece of iron being lowered into water as they sizzled through one beast after another.

Beast after beast felt the cold steel of Mary's blade as it cut through the air like the very wind itself. The carnage of the beasts marked Mary's path with pale bodies that lay hewn in an arc over the ice. The beasts took a heavy toll and began landing in droves, redirecting their attack on the ground. As they descended, it was as if the very sky itself was plummeting to the earth. They landed on the ice, filling the air with the sound of bone scratching bone as their talons dug deep into the ice. It took only moments for them to face together toward their target as they began to scratch their way straight toward Mary anxious to settle a debt long overdue.

Dorje leapt forward and swept her sword across the ice. The tiny flame that had lit the cavern just moments ago now burst out of the golden sword like a raging forest fire. The ice turned to vapor at the touch of the flame, creating a wide chasm of open water and separating Dorje and the oncoming beasts. The white creatures at the water's edge dug their talons in deep trying to stop their downward descent into the foreboding waters, but the beasts behind them had no such intent and the angry horde emptied into the icy water. Many were pushed deep into its depths by their brethren that piled in from behind.

John grabbed Dorje from behind and climbed onto the stone shore that marked the lake's end. Mary followed close behind. John and Franz had already made their way toward a dark stone passageway that had been carved into the cavern's mighty wall. They raced along the narrow passageway that was barely wide enough for John to squeeze through. Now propelled by blind hate, the white beasts continued to pile into the frozen waters of the lake, forming a floating bridge from those that had already been forsaken in the cold waters. Over this bridge of freezing flesh they sped toward the passageway. John turned and held his ground deep within the hall but he was still able to see the beasts at the other end. They beat against the pathway, shoving beast after beast into the narrow hall like an angry child hammering a square peg into a round hole, but the beasts were too large to pass. Those in the front screeched their last breaths as they scraped their talons on the smooth stone that separated them from their hard earned prey. But they could go no farther. John ran his hand along the smooth wall beside him, wondering if those who had carved this wonderful path had carved it only this wide for the very reason of keeping these beasts out. He turned and ran toward the dim light of Dorje's sword that was now far up the path.

When John caught up with the group, they were standing at the foot of a winding stair that disappeared up into the darkness. Max had an arrow pointed down the hall that John had just passed through. "How far back are the beasts?"

John bent over trying to catch his breath. "They were too wide to fit into the path." John then looked down at Dorje. "It was your sword that saved us all."

Dorje blushed. "The sword seemed to move on its own."

Mary nodded. "I know that feeling. You are with us for a reason, Dorje. You have been chosen to follow our path. The blade you carry will only be wielded by the one who is chosen for it."

Mary now held her sword over her shoulder as she spoke. Dorje smiled and held her sword in a similar fashion.

CHAPTER 46

Kytann's Brother

Dorje was the first to climb the stairs with her sword to light the way. John took the rear, as the path was narrow and none could have seen the light if they were behind him.

They climbed for over an hour before the path opened into a great hall lined with gold. Max drew an arrow and kept it at the ready on his bow. John and Mary stood close by, ready to strike whatever awaited them. Franz stood off in the shadows away from the golden carvings, guarding their flank with knives in hand. Dorje led the group into the golden hall.

As the light of her sword passed through the hall, small flames ignited from the nostrils of golden dragons carved into the walls. The flames emerged as silver dust and they blew from the nostrils of the golden beasts, covering the floor and all who passed by. The hall was massive like a cathedral. Even the brightness of Dorje's light could not penetrate the deep darkness that hung from on high. As they looked back, the long hall glowed in golden light that sparkled in the silver dust that lay like a deadly carpet over the hall's floor.

Dorje finally reached the end of the light from the walls. Ahead lay stairs spanning the width of the hall leading into an ominous shadow that would not yield its darkness to the flame of the sword. John now moved to the front with his halberd raised high and began to climb the steps.

A voice then entered into everyone's mind. "John, what is it that you seek that you should bring pain and death to this hall?"

John stopped and looked for the source of the voice but could only see darkness ahead. "We come in the name of the great bear to destroy the black tree."

The voice in their minds continued. "Desire for destruction brings you to the steps of my hall, but it is desire itself that threatens to destroy you all."

Max moved forward next to John, his arrow still drawn, pointing into the darkness. "I have heard such a voice in my mind before. It was the voice of a demon that had fallen from the light. Show yourself or I will end you with an arrow from the black tree."

Max's mind filled with the other's voice. "I see the tracks of my brother Kytann in your mind, Max. Like him I also grew tired of the war, but far earlier than he. He sought peace in solitude and I see that he received it at your hand. I seek a higher end, one beyond what your desires would allow you to see until now."

Max's mind went blank as if a dark cloud had descended upon him, and as he looked at the others he realized their minds had gone blank, too. The voice continued. "It is easiest to grasp the truth of reality in the deep of space. That is where I have brought your minds."

A strange disc came into view. It was round like a warrior's shield with a concave center. It moved forward through the face of the shield pulling the very fabric of space into it as it traveled, forming what seemed like a wave of concentrated space. Its shape remained the same as it sped by them but it was clear to all that the translucent shield had no substance of its own but was instead only a density wave in the fabric of space itself. It rolled by them like a wave over the surface of the ocean and it was beautiful.

The voice continued. "The nature of this universe cannot be explained. It must be seen for its truth to be known. What you look at now is a solitary piece of light. As you can see, it is not a thing of substance but merely a wave in the darkness of the universe."

Their minds then filled with many such pieces of light that at first appeared to be moving in random, but over time they sensed a rhythm and harmony to their movement, like a silent dance kept in time to the harmony of the universe around them. Their view then expanded to see a great silver willow tree blowing in the breeze. As the scene slowed down they could see that the willow tree was like the pieces of light that flowed through the darkness as it moved. It did not exist as a permanent thing but was more like a wave in the ocean that kept its shape.

"This is the tree that you desire to destroy. But as you can now see for yourselves, the tree is only an illusion. It is not permanent as you imagined. It is part of the flow of the universe. It exists no more than a wave on the ocean exists. It exists only in your mind."

Their vision was brought back to the golden hall, but instead of seeing it as they did when they walked in they now saw it in the slow motion view that they saw the tree. Everything was in the state of motion, being broken down and recreated like the wave of light. As they looked down at their own bodies they could see that they were no different. What they thought of as solid bodies were actually complex waves moving through the darkness of the universe.

"As you can now see, even what you considered to be yourself is not real. You are an illusion in your own mind. You are no more than a wave in darkness."

Their view then expanded out to see the entire valley. They saw mountains and waterfalls dancing with lush trees and tall grasses nearby. The rhythm and the harmony of the dance were beautiful. They then looked at themselves within that picture and saw that they stuck out, disrupting the smooth flow of the wavelike scenery that passed by.

"The flow of these waves is all that exists. There is no meaning outside of the harmony of the wave. The most any of us can hope for is to find our way back into that harmony. It is your desires that prevent you from finding harmony with the universe … desires for things that are not real … that are only waves themselves. You have been living in an illusion. Your quest is an illusion. This place is for those who are ready to discard their desires and enter into harmony with the universe."

John looked down at his hand as he moved his fingers back and forth.

The voice then focused on John. "I see in your mind that you have seen this before. The one you know as a bear showed you the universe as it is."

John said nothing as he continued to move his fingers back and forth, watching them be recreated moment by moment.

"The one you know as a bear believes himself to be in control of the universe. This is also only an illusion. He sings his song to the harmony of the waves, but he does not create the waves in the universe. No one does."

The voice stopped for a moment and then resumed. "I had once sought to destroy the one you know as a bear, but I have abandoned that quest. It was my desire for his death that separated me from the harmony of the universe. I no longer seek to kill him, or you for that matter, because you do not exist."

John's vision returned to normal, his halberd held loosely at his side. The voice had shown him what Soman had shown him in the forest. He could imagine that he was nothing, and he felt despair as he realized he had seen himself in the slow motion of recreation before. But he could not imagine Soman as nothing. The thought of losing Soman left a dark hole in him, a hole he would crawl into and hide if he could.

The entire group was in a state of despair, their weapons hanging on their sides, all except for one. Franz leapt from the side, his bushy hair heavy laden with the silver dust of the room, and landed several steps up from John. With both knives in his hand he brought one low to the step. The heavy silence of the moment was brought to an end by the screeching of metal on stone. "I am the rider of the worms in the service of the great bear. I am afraid of no one."

The darkness at the top of the stairs receded and there lying on a red and gold carpet at the top was a giant snow leopard the size of Kytann, with powdery silver hair and eyes as black as night. The leopard did not so much as move as he lazily looked down upon Franz and spoke. "I am no one." And with that a trap door opened under Franz and he disappeared down a dark chute.

* * * * *

Dorje jumped to the edge of the opening. "What have you done with the boy?"

The leopard smiled. "He has gone to seek enlightenment, as has your father."

Dorje said nothing as she threw herself into the chute. Jolted back to reality, the rest of the group followed Dorje. The chute was cool and smooth hewn from the rock of the mountain. Dorje felt herself speeding up as the chute wound its way down the mountain. She tried to push herself down faster and faster. Her mind was filled with the hope of seeing her father again, wherever this path ended. She saw a small light at the end of the tunnel, which she was quickly approaching.

* * * * *

Franz sat on a cool bed of green grass. His great mop of hair sparkled with silver specks like a diamond crown on his head in the bright sunlight. Looking around him he was overcome with the lush green valley that he had fallen into. Rolling hills of tall grass with fruit trees covered all that the eye could see, bordered by the white of the mountains which held the valley like two cupped hands holding a precious jewel. Colors seemed brighter than what he had remembered and everything sparkled as if it were encrusted with small diamonds. It was what he would have imagined paradise would look like. The only things within his sight that did not sparkle were a small river that ran through the middle of the valley which was fed from the underground lake above and a hole in a nearby rock through which Dorje was presently being shot out like a cannon ball toward his present position. Franz took evasive action and moved to the side as Dorje tumbled onto the grass beside him. The others soon followed.

Mary was the first to get up from the grass. Like the others, she sparkled as if she had been hewn from a solid diamond. The beauty of the valley was overwhelming, so much so that she wept at its sight. As the others arose, their hearts were relieved from their heavy burdens and their thoughts were consumed with the beauty of the valley. That is, all but Franz, who sparkled less than the others, or at least what you could see of him. His great mop of hair kept most of the silvery dust from adorning his skin. He stood at the ready now with knives in hand looking for the black tree.

John stood and rested the tip of his halberd into the soft soil below. It sunk as if it had been planted in hot butter two feet into the ground and there he left it as he went to examine the fruit growing on a nearby pear tree. Max followed suit by laying down his bow near the halberd and went to join John. Mary and Dorje left their weapons in the grass and went to pick raspberries, as both were very hungry.

Franz could not believe his eyes as he saw his companions drifting about the valley like so many honey bees searching for nectar. He went to

John under the pear tree. "We can eat later, Father. The tree is nearby. I can feel it in the soil. We must hurry. It will be dark in only an hour and we will be exposed."

John looked down at Franz as if he were crazy. "Did you hear nothing of what the leopard said? Our quest was like dust in the wind. Calm yourself and eat." John plucked a pear from the tree and as the branch shook, silver dust showered down on John and Max. They ate and then quickly fell asleep under the tree.

Franz shook John but he was fast asleep with a wide smile on his face. Max was the same. Franz was infuriated and stabbed the fruit tree in the trunk. His blade sunk deep into the wood, allowing his closed fist to hit the trunk hard. He pulled out his knife and rubbed his hand. It was odd that the knife should sink so deep into a tree, he thought. His blade was the same as the other ones. They were only sharp when cutting through something evil. He looked up at the pear tree. It had no evil appearance to it.

Franz went to find Mary and Dorje, who were now sleeping next to a raspberry bush. Frustrated beyond words, he kicked the bush and a cloud of silvery dust rose and settled on the girls. Franz's eyes then opened wide as he felt dirty for the first time in his life. He slowly retracted his arms in under the protection of his great bush of hair and stepped away from the bush very slowly. He knew he was right to feel threatened in this place. He looked off to the west. The sun had already drifted behind the mountain. He did not have much time left before he lost the light of day. For a moment he felt very alone, but then he remembered that he was not alone. There was one other on the journey who had not lost his senses. He began to sing the song that John had taught him that told of the greatness of Soman, the song that John had used to open the narrow path of the forest. Franz's heart lightened as he sang.

He ran back to the grass where the girls had left their swords. He picked up Dorje's sword, but the flame would not light. It was as he feared. The sword would only light for Dorje, the one the sword had picked. He picked up both of the weapons and ran to the river and set them beside it. He then ran back toward Dorje and picked her up carefully so as to get as little of the silvery dust on himself as possible. Over his shoulder he carried her to the river and waded into the water. Unlike the warmth of the valley the water was cold and bit hard on the skin. He then submerged Dorje in the water as he sang his song. The cold water washed away the silvery dust from her body and she awoke with a start.

"Where is my family?" She then pushed away from Franz. "Why are we standing in the middle of the river?"

Franz smiled but looked a little hurt. "You were put to sleep by the silvery dust that covers everything here. The water has washed you clean. It is how you woke up. Go grab your sword. We must wake the others. They are not safe. It is getting dark."

Dorje made her way to the bank of the river and picked up her sword. The flame at the end immediately lit bright, illuminating all around them in the silvery hue of the valley. She looked back at Franz. "We will never be able to carry the rest back to the river. They are too big to carry."

Franz nodded. It was a problem. As he looked around him he smiled, wading over to a lily pad that grew near the shore of the river. He submerged the pad and then lifted it up by the corners. A gallon of cold water lay trapped with the flower inside. Dorje understood and grabbed a lily pad herself. Together they carried their lily jugs of water back to the tree where John and Max had fallen asleep. Together they threw both pads of water on John's head. He woke with a start but was still groggy, speaking nonsense as if still deep within a dream. Franz and Dorje helped him up and guided him like a blind horse to the water, where they threw him in the river. He submerged like a giant melon and then floated down the river several yards with his head still submerged. Franz started inching toward the water, beginning to worry that John would not wake up and would drown. As if hearing his thoughts, John exploded with consciousness, his arms and legs flailing in the water. Once his head was out of the water Franz called to him and John swam to the riverside looking at Franz and Dorje in awe.

"What happened? I do not remember going near a river."

Dorje took a rod from the riverbank and struck a patch of grass nearby. A cloud of silvery dust arose from the grass and drifted down over the river. "That changed the way we thought and made us grow tired. It stole away desire."

John nodded. It was then that he noticed that it was dark and a chill ran through his spine. "Where are Mary and Max?"

The howl of some beast echoed through the valley. Franz and Dorje began to run up the bank and John followed. They arrived at Mary first and John hefted her over his shoulder. Next they went to Max. Franz dragged him out from under the tree, not wanting to risk having John covered with the silvery powder that covered its branches. Once away from the tree John picked up Max and flung him over his other shoulder. Together the three ran back to the river with Dorje leading the way. Once at the river, John waded out into the water and submerged Mary and Max. Within several minutes everyone had returned to their senses. In the distance a great howl could be heard. Whatever was out there was getting closer.

CHAPTER 47

The Five-Eyed Beasts

John looked around him as he stood waist high in the river. The world glowed a silvery white, lit by the flame of Dorje's sword, beautiful but deadly. Whatever beasts that lived near the black tree were beginning to awaken. There would be no waiting for dawn to attack the tree this time. Whatever happened, it would have to happen tonight. He looked back at the shore covered in silvery dust. They would not make it a hundred yards in the tall grass without being covered in the dust again. He could see Franz carrying down his halberd and Max's bow. He was the only one with any defense from the dust. He chuckled at the thought of Franz's bushy hair saving them all. He could not count how many times he had tried to convince Franz to cut it down. No more. Franz could keep his hair as long as he wanted.

John then looked down at the river. It was the only clean part of the valley. He motioned Franz and Dorje to join them back in the water. They would travel in the river for as long as they could. They did not know where they were going and so they decided to walk with the current. It seemed that more of the valley lay in that direction and it would be an easier walk. The river bottom was of compact sand which made the river an easy choice.

As they walked, John scanned the riverbanks for any sign of life, but none was to be found. He saw lily pads growing here and there and gathered them in under his arm when he found them. To his reckoning he would need at least six or seven. He saw Max's shadow on the water with an arrow on his bow. Everyone was on edge. The dark field that protected the last black tree was clearly on the minds of all, all except for John. The vision that the leopard had shown him of the world now lay heavy on his heart, and yet there was something wrong, something that he was missing.

The riverbanks were now lined by trees laced with the silvery powder. The sight was one of the most beautiful things that John had ever seen. It reminded him of the tree line in the foggy moonlight of his dreams of old. Without thinking he began looking for the great bear in the tree line of the riverbank. He found himself missing Soman. He remembered how Soman had restored his life after he had nearly burned to death. He remembered when he had first shown him the great song.

The song … it was then that it struck him that the vision the leopard implanted in their minds was correct in all respects except for the song. He had felt the rhythm and the harmony of the universe passing by him but he had not heard the song that drove the process. He concentrated back in the depths of his memory. He remembered the world flowing from one moment of creation to the next, and then he remembered seeing Soman in the background. As the singer of the song he did not change from moment to moment. He was not part of the flow, not part of the song. He was the source. *The leopard is so close to the truth and yet he is infinitely separated from it.* John longed for Soman now more than ever. But there was no sign of the great bear in the tree line. The howls of beasts were getting closer.

For two hours they walked down the cold river. Dorje's light was bright, but it still only lit up the banks and at most a hundred yards to either side. If the dark tree did not lie on the bank of the river they could walk right past it and never know better. John began to smell the fetid breath of the cursed beasts. The howls had stopped but he suspected that they were close by. Time was running out. To his left he saw a clearing on the bank. There was a stone landing and at the back edge of the landing was a pole with several strings attached to it. John followed the strings down to the ground where they ended in a pile of the silvery powder with a small skeleton of a bird the size of a chicken. Fist sized stones surrounded the pile of powder and bones. The others noticed nothing but had also smelled the nearby stench of the fowl beasts of the night and had their weapons at the ready.

John took a few more steps down the river and then stopped in his tracks. His companions froze and searched the tree line on the opposite bank, but John's eyes floated back to the stone landing. What was it that the old man in the cave had kept repeating? "Silvery stones and chicken bones." That could not be coincidence. John made haste toward the stone landing and the others followed closely.

Max was now scanning the opposite tree line frantically. "What did you see, John? Where are they?"

John said nothing as he slowly walked up the stone landing toward the pile of silvery powder and chicken bones. "Silvery stones and chicken bones."

Dorje moved her way to the front and knelt down near the pole that had the string tied to it. She pulled up the string, which was still attached to the bony neck of a chicken. "This is string that my father and I made. These are some of the chickens that we took into the mountains with us. He was here." She passed the flame of the sword in an arch toward the nearby tree line. At first they saw nothing, but as they stared they could make out a small stone path that led from the river into the trees ahead.

John stood and pointed his halberd toward the path. "That is our path."

At those words the group heard a great noise on the opposite bank of the river. Three dog-like beasts with oily brown fur broke through the trees and began to bound through the water. They were each as tall as a house, with muscles that rippled tight over the span of their bodies. Their mouths were filled with two rows of razor sharp teeth. Each beast's head had five eyes that glowed red in the silvery night. The company of five needed no urging as they sprinted toward the opposite tree line.

John began throwing lily pads to his companions as they ran. One flopped on Mary's head. She looked back at John, clearly irritated. John smiled and threw one on his own head, creating a giant hood that draped over his shoulders. Mary looked at him as if he were crazy. The ground now shook as the giant beasts bounded toward them on this side of the shore. John pointed up at the branches of the trees. The branches shook with each leap of the craven beasts raining down silver powder below. Mary nodded, understanding what the lily pads were for, and made sure the others had their lily pads over their heads to keep the powder from fogging their brains.

When they reached the tree line a small path could be seen. All but Max slipped into the forest. Max turned and took aim with a black arrow and let loose. Without Dorje's light all he could see was the glowing red of the beast's eyes. He stood and watched for only a moment, but he saw one of the red eyes go dark and then heard the chilling howl of the wounded beast. Max turned and made haste down the path that could now only barely be seen from Dorje's light far ahead. The beasts' stampede had stopped. They would not follow them into the forest, but Max knew they would be back. The cursed beasts were killing machines. Thousands of years on the hunt had taught them the value of patience. He would need to be wary when they hit a clearing, which he knew in his heart was inevitable.

The path through the trees was quiet. Franz had placed a lily pad on top of his head, but it was far too small to cover the width of his hair. It was like trying to use a napkin for a tablecloth, he told himself. The humor was lost, though, at the site of the pile of silvery powder that was accumulating on the pad. Mary looked all around at the trunks of trees that surrounded them separated by falling powder that looked like snow bathed in the moonlight. Where was all this powder coming from?

Dorje led the way and started slowing her pace. Ahead the group could see the trees thinning. The cover of the trees would soon be at an end. As they neared the last tree they looked across a grassy field and in the distance they could see a giant willow tree with lotus blossoms covering its long stringy branches. A cloud moved off of the moon overhead and they could see a breeze blowing the giant tree and unleashing the silvery powder from its blooms.

None had to be told that the tree that they were looking at was the black tree that they sought. It glowed with a supernatural light in the radiance of the moon. Its long rope like vines swayed loosely in the breeze as if to invite those watching to come take rest under their protection. The daydream of sleepily lounging in the comfort of the willow broke suddenly at the fetid smell of the cursed beasts. They were not within sight but they were near.

John motioned Dorje to hold her sword low. The flame subsided to only a tiny flicker. The moon lit the open field as bright as if they were there in the light of day. They saw the stone path cutting through the field in a straight line. There was no cover other than the tall grass itself. John motioned everyone to stoop as low as they could. He then moved out toward the field, bent low in the naked moonlight.

The group hit the path running as low as they could go. John poked his head up over the grass line but could see nothing but the waving fields of grass and a large formation of rocks about a hundred yards ahead. Perhaps the rocks could be used as cover when the beasts showed themselves. As if to mock this thought, fourteen red eyes opened in what he had thought were rocks and began to charge their position.

John now stood tall looking in both directions. There was nowhere to run. He looked back toward the tree line. Maybe they could make it, but then what? The ground shook with the first onslaught of the beasts.

There was only one choice, and Franz had already committed to the only option left to them. He leapt up to see over the grass. The beasts were advancing on them straight up the course of the path. Silver dust flew everywhere, making the beasts appear to be running within a cloud that circled their feet. Franz leapt high in the air down the path, each leap carrying him twenty yards farther. His open attack seemed to infuriate the beasts as they howled at him. Franz now heightened his leaps, paying close attention to the timing. One of the three cursed beasts had a huge crater in the side of its head where Max had wounded it with a black arrow. It lagged behind the other two, wobbling as it ran as if drunk. He would leave that one to Max. Looking ahead Franz saw his last launching point like a target on the path. He made contact with bent legs and then exploded into the air. The beast leading the charge paused for a moment but it was too late. Franz landed on the snout of one of the beasts and quickly dug in both knives to secure himself for what promised to be a wild ride.

The beast wailed as its flesh was punctured by the blades. It moved its head frantically, trying to shake loose the unwanted parasite. Franz's legs whipped free in the open air of the night, but his hands held tight to his knives that were firmly secured into flesh and bone. Franz smiled as he was whipped from side to side. At the arc of the whip he noticed that he was being flung more slowly than when the beast's head bent downward. Timing out these precious moments, he quickly pulled out one knife and replanted it a little higher, climbing up to the beast's five glowing eyes. When he had reached the center of the eyes he let himself hang down over the center eye. He then pulled out one of his knives and pointed to an emblem of the great bear on his chest. The beast roared in anger but was helpless to stop what would follow.

Franz took his free knife and carved a hole the size of himself on the front of the eye. The piece that he cut fell away and glowing red gel erupted from the opening, covering Franz from head to toe. He took one swing back and then on the inward swing pulled his other knife free and flung himself into the glowing red eye. The flesh that he landed on was moist and covered with a syrupy fluid. Franz trudged to the back of the eye and dug his knives in deep again, carving out a portal in the beast.

* * * * *

Max could not believe his eyes as he saw Franz springing toward the beasts. As Franz leapt upon the leading beast, Max pulled back an arrow and let it fly toward the next beast in line. The arrow struck true in its head, creating a great crater of ash. Max pulled back another arrow and let it fly, concentrating on the same beast, as Mary, John, and Dorje ran past him.

Mary now held her sword up high, Dorje mimicking her by her side. It did not take long for the threesome to meet the gruesome beasts in battle. The three beasts bore down on Mary first. Her sword parried with lightning speed and sliced deeply into the jaw of one of the beasts. Dorje similarly brought down a mighty blow. Fire streamed from her sword as it cut deep into the flesh of the beast's foreleg. Like a table that had just lost a leg it toppled for a moment before gaining balance on its three good legs. John hammered down hard with his ax blade and sliced off half of the monster's lame foot. The beasts came at them again and again, all the while being pelted with black arrows that landed on their bodies like asteroids hitting the moon and creating ash laden craters that now covered the surface of all the beasts.

The half drunken beast in the rear now lay dead in the silvery grass beside the path. The beast with five remaining eyes made one last attack. Mary's blade found purchase deep within the beast's neck and it crumpled to the ground, its head falling on the path itself.

The last beast standing seemed to have no interest in the fight and circled and moaned in the tall grass as if overtaken with madness. Mary and the group watched from the path as the monster gyrated a contorted dance, clawing at its own head and ripping flesh and bone. As the beast rose high, its head silhouetted in the light of the full moon, Franz emerged at the crown of the beast's skull, having cut a hole from the inside. He shined in the moonlight, waist high into the beast, with both hands raised high in triumph, his blades gleaming. The beast convulsed as if struck in the back, whipping its head backward. Franz's glistening body flew out of the head like a cannon ball landing in the tall grass far from the path. An explosion of silver powder erupted on his impact.

The cursed beast twirled once and then fell far from the path but the others barely noticed, their eyes on the silvery cloud that marked Franz's impact in grassy field. Mary's eyes widened as she cried out in agony. She began to run toward where Franz had fallen but John grabbed her before she entered the tall grass. With tears in his eyes he raked his halberd through the grass creating a thick cloud of the silvery dust. None of them would make it more than ten yards into the grass before being overtaken by the intoxicating powder.

They all stood in silence and stared at the small cloud in the middle of the field. Then like a spear being thrown by a mighty warrior, Franz lunged out of the cloud and bounded toward the group. It was a spectacular sight as he exploded from spot to spot, leaving a heavy silver cloud with every leap. Each time he jumped he seemed to be getting heavier, and he sparkled in the moonlight as if he himself were the starry night. Franz landed hard on the path, covered head to toe with several inches of the deadly powder, but it seemed to have no effect on him. Even his hair was caked with silver, with only his eyes showing through his powdery coating.

Mary looked down on him with tears in her eyes but dared not touch him. How had he not succumbed to the heavy sleep of the powder? Max looked closer and ran the tip of his bow through Franz's powder coating. Underneath the powder the bow pulled out a stringy glob of gel from the beast's eye that coated Franz from head to toe. Mary looked at Max and both nodded, understanding that Franz's gel coating prevented the powder from touching his skin. Mary then walked to the beast's head that now lay in their path and cut a hole in its eye as Franz had done. The same gel poured out of the eye covering Mary in a sticky blanket that glistened in the moonlight. The others understood and stood in front of an eye as Mary cut a hole in each of the eyes in order to cover her companions with the same gel. John then led the party over the head of the dead beast and down the path toward the giant willow tree that now whipped and whirled in the wind as if to taunt the warriors of the great bear deeper into its lair.

CHAPTER 48

Dorje's Father

The path led to the side of the hanging vines of the massive tree. Long ropelike limbs hung down from the sky and seemed to stretch out beyond sight. Each vine was heavily laden with lotus blossoms which poured out the silvery powder like water from ten thousand fountains. The ropelike branches writhed like snakes as the group got closer. Ahead of the path lay a wide opening in the branches with thousands of the snakelike ropes squirming in the deadly tunnel formed for their passage. Mary took courage and began to walk into the tunnel. As soon as she placed one foot under the branches a rope whipped in and touched her on the cheek. She froze with the contact to the tree and as the rope departed she fell to the ground. John and Max pulled her away from the tree and laid her on the path in front of them. Several minutes later she returned to consciousness still groggy from the experience. John ran his finger over her gel covered cheek. There was a scar where the tree had pushed through the gel and touched her skin. They would need to take care not to touch the black tree. It was as it had been with the first black tree—to touch the bark was death. He wondered if the near fatal attack on Mary was meant as a warning from the tree. Be that as it may, they would never make it through the wide path provided by the tree alive. They would need to find another way in.

John stepped back and examined the wall of rope that hung so densely from the sky. It had a familiar feel to it. It was not unlike the dense forest that bordered his old home. He then smiled as an idea crept into his head. John led the group into the thick grass along the border of the tree. The tree would not suspect an attack away from its own entrance. Who before them would have even been able to walk through the grass to another site? He took his companions far down and around the circumference of the tree and when he could no longer see the path he turned toward the deadly wall of branches and began to sing. Without a further thought he stepped into the branches and the narrow path opened as it had in the forest.

John ran with a slow jog as they all made their way through thousands of the vines that now parted for them like a curtain perpetually opening on stage. John wondered whether the tree could feel the narrow path through its own branches, but it mattered not. They had only one way to go and that was forward. As the branches thinned they could see at first hundreds and then thousands of skeletons of men and women sitting cross-legged on the ground with cones of powder resting on their skulls. Dorje looked with concern as they passed by pilgrim after pilgrim whose desires had been put to sleep once they were under the poisonous powder of the black tree. As they came closer some of those sitting on the ground had not yet fallen into death. Their eyes glazed over as if they were in a deep trance staring at the massive trunk of the black tree that loomed ahead.

Dorje was no longer looking ahead but instead at the faces of those still living under the spell of the tree. Abruptly she stopped as she pointed out toward one of the tree's captives.

"That is my father!" Dorje began to step out of the narrow path but Max caught her and shook his head.

"We will find him later. To leave the narrow path is certain death."

Dorje said nothing for a moment staring at her father, and then, mustering all the strength she had in her, she nodded. John knew she wanted to try to save her father no matter what the cost. But he could see on the child's face that she had decided to trust in her companions. She would have patience.

They were now only feet away from the tree when John's toe caught the tip of a root coming out from the ground. He flung his halberd out in front of him to catch him from falling into the trunk of the black tree. The spearhead of the halberd sunk deep into the flesh of the black tree and the branches around them appeared to awake to the presence of their enemy. John rotated as he fell. Not wanting to touch the bark, he reached out with one hand to break his fall trying to reach the ground below. On his way down a single finger brushed against the trunk of the tree, and there he froze.

John no longer saw the tree or his companions—only the world as the leopard had shown him in the golden hall. Time slowed as he again looked down at his own body as it flowed in harmony with the universe that was displayed around him. The great weight of despair clutched at his heart tighter than it had in the hall. The tree absorbed like a sponge nearly all the desire he had left within him, nearly all hope. But in his mind he was still singing the song that had opened the narrow path only minutes before. The song reminded him of his strongest desire, that for Soman. With that thought his heart warmed and the deep despair fell away like charred flesh. Then in the back of his mind he could faintly hear the great song of Soman that made and remade the universe moment by moment. What John saw in front of him did not change in one sense, but in another sense it was totally reformed. The harmony of the flowing universe could now be seen as obeying the will of its master. It was as if full color that no human eye had ever seen had been washed upon a charcoal sketch of the universe. John saw great stars and galaxies pirouette and fall to the harmony of the song of songs, and hope returned to his heart.

* * * * *

Mary watched as John fell toward the tree and she froze. If a tree can become angry, it is in a rage right now, she thought, as a flurry of vines headed straight toward them. Mary raised her sword and the others retreated behind her. The first wave of vines came in from above and Mary's sword cut them all to the quick. The vines recoiled as they felt the sting of the blade. She could see more vines being recruited from all directions and realized the first attack had only been a test. Up high she heard a sound like the crack of a whip and all of the vines shot like lightning toward their position. Mary doubted that the sword could handle all of the vines but she held it up high. Dorje jumped out in front of Mary and held her sword up to the sky. The flame at the edge of Dorje's sword grew brighter and brighter. Soon a ball of flame engulfed Dorje and Mary and those behind them. They could feel the flames licking their skin but felt no pain. It was a different story for the vines that entered the sword's inferno. As they passed into the flame they instantly turned to ash, which rained down on the group like snow. The tree seemed to become more frantic as more vines burned and sent an unending army of the deadly vines toward Dorje, but none was able to penetrate the flame.

* * * * *

Franz looked down at where John's finger was touching the trunk. The skin on his finger was turning black. Franz knew what needed to be done. He raised one of his knives and cut the finger off. John awoke from his trance and looked down at Franz, not knowing what had just happened. Franz tipped his knife from his forehead as if to say, "You're welcome." He then pointed to the halberd and then John returned to his senses. Pulling the halberd out of the tree, he swung it around and chopped deep within the wood with the ax blade. Above, the tree seemed to moan, but John was now a man on a mission and heard nothing.

* * * * *

Mary saw what John was doing and remembered why they had come. She went back to the trunk of the tree and began slicing huge sections of wood from where John was chopping. They made good pace and Dorje's flame provided them the protection they needed. Max saw the vines now frantically waving back and forth as if they had gone mad. One vine in its madness knocked over one of the nearby skeletons and bones flew into the fire, but they were not burned landing near Dorje's feet. The vines stopped their motion for a moment and then began to grab hundreds of nearby skeletons and whipped them hard toward Dorje and her blade. Max grabbed Dorje and pulled her in under the portion of the trunk that Mary and John had chopped into. The bones shattered at the base of the trunk like a bomb exploding, with sharp splinters attacking all in sight from the point of impact.

* * * * *

The trunk of the tree began to creak as its weight searched for strength to uphold its enormous girth. Dorje now scanned over the people sitting on the ground, passing over face after face until her eyes froze on one in particular. The tree seemed to sense the connection immediately. A vine dropped down from the sky and wrapped around her father's neck. The vine yanked up, hanging the man ten feet in the air. The man writhed in agony both from being hung as well as from being touched by the bark of the vine.

Dorje knelt down and the ball of flame dimmed as she began to lose heart. The tree was offering a trade, a trade she could not refuse. Before the ball of flame shrank low enough to expose her, Max loosed an arrow, slicing the vine in two, and her father fell free to the ground. The ball of flame grew as Dorje saw her father freed, but the black tree was not finished. Four vines now shot out toward the man. Each vine grabbed hold of an arm or a leg and now raised the man high with his limbs stretched far apart. *The tree's going to tear him apart.* Dorje was filled with despair.

It was then that the flame went out. Max took aim at the vines holding the man and cut one after another with his arrows, but with the flame gone the vines ignored the man, dropping him to the ground, and shot out toward Max and Dorje. Max loosed arrow after arrow blindly into the oncoming vines but there were too many. The vines grabbed Max first, then Dorje, and threw them far from the trunk. Max could feel the burn from where the vine had grabbed his ankle but it did not hold on long. The tree felt its weight shifting. Its target was now John.

John was deep within the trunk of the tree. Mary had quit chopping and now cut at the advancing vines, trying to pull John and herself out from the trunk. Mary's sword swung down hard and cut twenty vines as they advanced, but three caught her ankle and whipped her fifty feet out from the trunk. She landed near Max, who was running toward where Dorje had fallen. Max picked up Mary on his way. Dorje ran toward her father, who lay still on the ground. Mary and Max lifted the man off the ground and draped him over their shoulders. They looked back at the trunk and saw splinters fly. Franz was still deep within the trunk holding back the vines with his knives. John pulled back his halberd and took one more giant stroke at the trunk, and with that blow the tree began to twist as it leaned toward Mary and Max.

John and Franz jumped out from the base of the trunk just before the weight of the tree collapsed down, crushing the spot they had just been standing in. The tree was still for a moment and then began to list to the left. The sky moaned as the canopy above gave way.

"Run!" Max yelled. He and Mary took Dorje's father and began to run with Dorje at their side. They ran straight for the trunk wanting to be on the other side before the massive tree hit the ground. As they passed the trunk they could see the vines rushing into the sky as the tree tipped, pulling them with it. A faint horizon could now be seen under the raised vines and they ran like wild deer for the newfound opening.

John and Franz were now well ahead of them and had just made it out from under the shadow of the tree. The ground shook as the massive trunk struck the earth and tons of dead vines rose up in the air and then came raining down on the shadow of the tree. Mary and Max dove forward with the old man in tow and landed in the dirt with the heft of the vines falling just behind them at their feet. Dorje ran to her father, who looked very pale.

The old man opened one eye and smiled. "Dorje, my child." The man coughed. "I do not have long to tell you this. I am sorry, Dorje, for bringing you here." The man then looked up toward Mary, who he had seen carrying him out from under the tree. He saw the emblem of the great bear on her shoulder and felt it. "Take care of my daughter. Take her to the bear, the bear who saved me from the darkness in my dreams. He promised me peace from the emptiness that imprisoned me. It is to him that I now go." He then looked back at Dorje. "Goodbye, my child, I leave you in the care of the great bear." And with that the man breathed his last breath.

CHAPTER 49

The Void

As the black tree fell to the ground, the mountain shook. The leopard awoke in the dark, sensing what had happened. He looked down the golden hall that lay before him awaiting his freedom from this world, a freedom that had called for him for thousands of years. There at the end of the dark hall he saw two bright white eyes that he knew from days long past. He no longer had the desire to run, to kill, to love. Such motives were beneath him and beyond his reach. He sought only the harmony of the universe that he saw with his waking eyes.

The flames lit in the dragons' nostrils as the great bear strode down the golden hallway. His fur gleamed in the firelight like a majestic robe. "Long have you waited to be free of me, to merge with the creation." There was a sadness in the great bear's voice as he spoke. The words carried a sense of great personal loss and betrayal. "Tonight you will be given that for which you have longed for ... to leave my presence and to be immersed in the void."

The leopard saw Soman approaching. The hall he saw as a never ending wave of the universe, but Soman glowed with an eternal light that did not regenerate from moment to moment. It was then that he heard the song of songs that created all things and a piece of him understood the depth of the sentence being imposed upon him.

Soman rose up on his hind legs and spread his arms. A great blinding light emitted from him and through him. "Let it be as you wish."

* * * * *

At that moment the leopard's body went limp and his spirit was vanquished to the dark of the void. There he was enveloped in the silence of the dark where he neither felt, nor heard, nor saw anything but the deep darkness of the never ending void. The harmony he had sought was gone, as it was only a product of the song of the bear, which he had strived for so long to be rid of. The beautiful ebb and flow of the waves of the universe were gone. He was now left to the dark of the void, as it was before the song had been sung. There he wallowed in the emptiness of the nothingness that he had for so long sought. His soul cried out to be heard but there was no sound, only the emptiness of the void.

CHAPTER 50

Cleansed at the River

At the death of Dorje's father a great wind swept down and swirled around Dorje and her father. The wind grew in intensity as it gusted through the valley, carrying with it the silvery powder. With tears in her eyes Dorje watched with amazement as the wind swept the valley clean, carrying the silvery powder away deep into the mountains. Dorje looked up to Mary, to whom her father had left her, but did not know what to say. Mary knelt down and held her and together they buried him where he lay.

The only powder left in the valley was the powder caked on the gel on their bodies that the wind did not carry away. They walked solemnly back up the path to the stone landing from where they had emerged from the river. John did not know any songs fit for a wake, and so he sang the only song he knew, the song that the bear had taught him. As he waded into the water, the water danced around in rhythm with the song, scrubbing his body clean.

Mary was the next to enter the water. The water ran past her as it normally had and the silver gel clung tight to her body. She looked at John and he motioned her to come closer. He placed his hand on her head and pushed her under the water, all the while singing. The water swirled and frothed around Mary in rhythm to the song and when she arose she was clean.

Max was next. He looked nervous as he entered the water. John motioned him to come near. Max, his body covered head to toe with the gel of a giant's eye and the evil powder that clung tight to his body, looked at John. "I know it is Soman who swirls the water to clean away the evil that clings tight to our bodies, but it will not work for me, I do not deserve it. I fired the arrow at him in the forest. How can the favor of Soman ever rest upon me?"

John smiled and held out his hand. Max allowed himself to be submerged. At first there was no swirling of the water. Max looked up at John from under the water, but John only smiled and continued to sing. Max's lungs burned from lack of breath. His mind began to grow dim, his breath now fully gone, and as he reached the very edge of desperation he asked for what he knew he did not deserve, forgiveness. Under his arms he felt something pulling. He looked down but only saw the froth of the swirling water as it lifted him out of the river twirling him high in the air as it washed him clean for all to see. Across the river hidden in the trees on the opposite bank sat the great bear with a tear in his eye as he looked on.

Franz was next. Franz had no hesitation as he bounded from the bank to John's side. John put his hand on the silver crust that covered Franz's thick bush of hair. He lowered his hand into the water wondering how even the power of Soman would be able to clean the gel caked powder from all that hair. For Franz there was no swirling but instead an explosion of water that left a small crater in the riverbed. The water blast had thrown Franz high in the air. He fell back into the water next to John cleaner than he had ever been. From the woods across the bank the great bear laughed so hard he fell over.

Dorje now stood alone on the bank covered with the silvery gel. She looked back toward where they had buried her father as if to say goodbye and then slowly walked into the water. When she arrived at John she looked up at his massive body and he could see the fear on her face. He smiled as he continued to sing. His hand lowered into the water and the water swirled and frothed around Dorje, tickling her as it passed over her body. When she arose she was clean.

The five of them now stood in the water with their weapons, looking at each other as if to ask, where are we to go next? John looked back toward where they had destroyed the black tree. Its stump now lay under tons of vines. It would take weeks or longer to dig down to it to find the next map.

It was then that the group heard a great rushing of water up river. They walked together down the riverbed to investigate the noise. The flow of the river picked up speed as they neared the noise. A rumbling sound could then be heard behind them. They looked back only in time to see a giant wave of water pushing through the river, which picked them up and carried them to the loud noise that had drawn them there. As they rode on top of the wave they could see ahead a great black hole into which the water raced. Dorje looked at the hole with fear, but Mary held her hand as they were swept into the darkness. The last to go was Franz, who was thrown high into the air by the wave. He did a double back flip with a twist and disappeared into the darkness of the hole.

And thus the adventures of John and his companions continued down the narrow path ...

Made in the USA
Lexington, KY
05 December 2015